"I never took you for a coward, Liam."

"Sometimes a clean break is best. The sole reason I came here was to be alone. The same's true for you. We were each doing fine, as long as we kept our distance. But it's not too late to reverse the damage."

"Not for you, perhaps."

"What's that supposed to mean, Janie? Are you saying you might wind up…?

"Pregnant? Isn't it a bit late for you to be asking me that?"

"*Could* you be pregnant?"

"I guess we'll just have to wait and see. If you happen to bump into me six months from now and I'm big as a house, you'll know—"

"Janie!" he exploded. "This isn't something to be taken lightly. If you find—"

"Don't worry, Liam, I won't come running to you, not when you've made your feelings so plain."

"Your being pregnant would change a lot of things."

CATHERINE SPENCER, once an English teacher, fell into writing through eavesdropping on a conversation about Harlequin romances. Within two months she changed careers and sold her first book to Harlequin in 1984. She moved to Canada from England thirty years ago and lives in Vancouver. She is married to a Canadian and has four grown children—two daughters and two sons—plus two dogs and a cat. In her spare time she plays the piano, collects antiques and grows tropical shrubs.

Books by Catherine Spencer

HARLEQUIN PRESENTS®
2101—THE UNEXPECTED WEDDING GIFT
2143—ZACHARY'S VIRGIN

Catherine Spencer

PASSION'S BABY

TORONTO • NEW YORK • LONDON
AMSTERDAM • PARIS • SYDNEY • HAMBURG
STOCKHOLM • ATHENS • TOKYO • MILAN • MADRID
PRAGUE • WARSAW • BUDAPEST • AUCKLAND

ISBN 0-373-12172-5

PASSION'S BABY

First North American Publication 2001.

Copyright © 2000 by Kathy Garner.

CHAPTER ONE

AFTERWARD, when it was too late to go back and do things differently, Jane looked for someone to blame for the chain of events which led to her first meeting with Liam McGuire.

Her grandfather topped the list, because he was the one who'd assured her, "You'll have our half of the island all to yourself this year. Steve's spending the summer with his married son in California."

But when she discovered that her grandfather's old fishing buddy hadn't bothered telling anyone he'd decided to rent his place to someone else while he was away, she tried shifting the blame to him. In all fairness though, Steve had the right to do as he pleased with his own property and, on top of that, was getting forgetful in his old age, so perhaps he couldn't be held accountable.

Of course, there was Liam McGuire himself, surely the messiest man ever born and one who needed to have someone wash out his mouth with soap to cure his bad language. The way he could curse would make a sailor blush! But again, if she were to be scrupulously objective, Jane had to admit that, as the legal tenant of Steve's house and with a signed lease to prove it, evil-tempered Liam McGuire was under no obligation to live up to her personal standards of socially acceptable behavior.

So, stymied on that front, also, she then tried blaming her dog. If Bounder hadn't had such a passion for wrapping his jaws around whatever was handiest and offering it as a gift to whomever he happened to meet, she might have been able to acquit herself with a modicum of dignity. On the other hand, if she'd done a better job of training him when he was a puppy, he wouldn't have developed such bad habits.

So, much though she loathed having to admit it, when all was said and done the blame ended up where it really belonged: squarely on her own shoulders. Which was why, in the middle of the morning on the first day of what was supposed to be her summer of spiritual and physical renewal, she found herself huddled behind a chunk of rock on the beach below the cottages, her face flaming with embarrassment and her heart staggering with shame.

"I'd have been better off staying in town," she muttered dolefully to Bounder, who alternated between fixing her in a meltingly sympathetic gaze and staring longingly at the waves breaking on the sand, forty yards away.

But the kind of serenity she craved wasn't to be found in the hectic bustle and pace of Vancouver's streets, so she'd returned to the haven of her childhood. Arriving at her grandfather's cottage late the previous night, she'd climbed the winding stairs to the big square room under the eaves, crawled under the goose feather quilt on the high brass bed, and fallen asleep to the sound of waves breaking on the shore and the smell of the sea filling her lungs.

For the first time in months, she had not been haunted by dreams. Instead, she'd slept deeply, certain that the tranquil solitude of Bell Island would cure what ailed her.

She'd woken early the next morning and, blissfully

unaware of the turmoil about to descend, had gone to the bedroom's north window to take in the view of Desolation Sound which defined the very essence of her happy childhood. But rather than deep blue waters snaking into quiet inlets against a backdrop of mountains, her attention had fastened on the thin column of smoke rising into the still air from the chimney next door.

Even then, she might have managed to avoid making such a colossal fool of herself if she hadn't also happened to notice the windows were still boarded up to protect them against the fury of the past winter's southeasterly gales. But it was now June, with summer arrived, which had made Jane very suspicious. Why would a legitimate occupant choose to live in semidarkness when every room in the place could be flooded with sunlight?

"There's something very fishy about this," she'd told Bounder. "I think we should investigate."

It had been an easy decision to make from the safety of her grandfather's cottage, but a twinge of uneasiness had fluttered down her spine as she approached the wraparound porch of the house. Suddenly, she'd been glad she had the eighteen-month-old Belgian sheepdog at her side.

The front door stood half open. Grasping Bounder by the collar, she'd knocked and called out, "Hello? Anybody there?"

But the shaft of light streaming through the open doorway revealed only dying embers in the fireplace, a pile of dirty dishes on the counter next to the sink, and a sweater flung carelessly over the back of the couch.

Somewhat reassured, she'd stepped fully inside to

take a closer look. A cell phone and a dozen or more books lay scattered haphazardly over the coffee table. Whoever had taken up residence obviously enjoyed reading, not to mention instant communication with the outside world.

But apart from a heap of clothes littering the floor beside an open canvas suitcase, and a sleeping bag and two pillows on the single mattress, the slivers of sunshine filtering between the cracks in the boards covering the bedroom windows gave away nothing of the occupant's identity beyond the fact that he wasn't trying to hide his untidy presence.

It had to be a "he," she'd reasoned. The sweater in the living room was too large for a woman and only a man would treat his clothes so carelessly or leave his sleeping bag in wrinkled disarray from a night's sleep.

"Still," she'd told Bounder, "whoever he is could at least have taken down the shutters and given the room a bit of natural light, not to mention a breath of fresh air. It's musty as a cellar in here."

By way of reply, Bounder had let out a low whine and pricked up his oversize ears, a clear signal that he'd heard someone approaching the house. Realizing her initial concern had crossed the boundary into outright infringement of privacy, Jane had made a beeline for the bedroom door, anxious at least to get as far as the living room before she was caught intruding. But the dog, tail thrashing in excitement, yanked himself free of her hold, snatched up the nearest piece of clothing, and raced ahead of her.

"Bounder, no!" she begged in an appalled whisper. "Oh, Bounder, please! Drop that! Give!"

She might as well have been speaking Swahili for all the attention he paid. Using his great paws as launching pads, he plowed on his merry way, leaving mayhem in his wake. She caught up with him on the far side of the living room sofa and had barely managed to rescue the item he'd filched from the bedroom when a shadow darkened the patch of sunlight shining across the floor from the open front door.

Straightening, she prepared to offer an introduction-cum-explanation for her uninvited presence. In fact, the words, "I'm Jane Ogilvie from next door and I just stopped by to say hello" were all ready to pop out of her mouth, but her attempt to appear nothing more than a friendly neighbor welcoming a summer visitor faltered and died before she uttered a single syllable.

The man had stationed himself on the cottage threshold, making escape impossible, and the cold, unwelcoming stare he directed at her would have silenced a thunderbolt. But it was neither the justifiable indignation in his eyes, which were the same translucent blue-green as the sea on a cold winter's day, nor the embarrassment of finding herself caught brazenly snooping through his home, that left her speechless. Instead she stared mutely at his legs, knowing she shouldn't, but unable to help herself.

From the way he let her squirm in the ensuing silence, it was her guess he was the kind who thrived on other people's discomfiture. Finally, when she was about ready to choke on humiliation, he said, in a voice so larded with bitterness that she recoiled, "What's the matter, Goldilocks? Never seen a man in a wheelchair before?"

Oh, yes, she could have told him, had he been at all interested in hearing her answer. But he was much too busy cursing with stunning vulgarity as he navigated the furniture and maneuvered himself farther into the room.

Knocking aside a wooden kitchen chair, he propelled himself around the table and only just missed wheeling over the tip of Bounder's tail in the process. "Move it, hound!" he snapped, not even pausing to consider that Bounder, had he been equally ill-tempered, could have taken a chunk out of his unshaven face.

Instead, the dog tried to lick the hand which clearly wouldn't have fed him if he'd been starving. Deciding sensitivity was wasted on such a man, Jane adopted a more confrontational approach. "Does the owner of this cottage know that you're living here?" she inquired, folding the garment she still held in her hand and fixing him in a forthright stare.

"What business is it of yours?" he shot back. "And what the devil do you think you're doing with my undershorts?"

She thought she'd already scaled the upper limit of human embarrassment but the realization that she was absently fingering underwear belonging to a man whose name she didn't even know taught her the folly of that assumption. "Uh…" she mumbled, switching her horrified gaze from his face to the scarlet maple leaves emblazoned on the offending garment. "Um…oh, dear, I didn't realize that's what these are."

"Cripes!" He rolled his rather beautiful eyes in disbelief. "You'll be telling me next that you didn't know you were trespassing on my property."

"But it's not your property," she said, latching onto any excuse to change the subject. "It belongs to Steve Coffey who is an old friend of my grandfather's and whom I've known since I was five years old." Then, realizing she still hadn't introduced herself, added,

"I'm Jane Ogilvie and I'm staying at the house on the other side of the cove."

"No, you're not," her ungracious host said flatly. "I'm Liam McGuire and when I signed the lease on this place, Coffey assured me I'd have the beach to myself all summer."

"Then we've both been misled, because my grandfather told me the same thing. But if you're worried I'm going to make a nuisance of myself, you can relax. I'm no more anxious to be neighborly than you are."

"Uh-huh." He looked pointedly at his boxer shorts. "Is that why you're having such a good time fiddling with my drawers?"

The flush which rode up her neck rivaled the underwear's maple leaves in color. "I most certainly am *not* fiddling...!"

"The hell you're not," he retorted with grim amusement. "The way you're stroking them is downright indecent. You'll be asking me to model them next."

She dropped them as hurriedly as if they'd suddenly caught fire. "I don't think so!"

"Why not?" he asked, his voice laced with slow insolence. "Because it's not polite to recognize that a man in a wheelchair exists below the waist?"

"No," she said, refusing to submit to that particular brand of emotional blackmail. "Because you're not my type."

"Why not?" he repeated in the same lazy drawl. "Because I'm in a wheelchair?"

"No. Because you're arrogant, unpardonably rude, about as unappealing as a cockroach, and apparently enjoy living in a pigsty."

He smiled. At least, she supposed his sudden display of flawless teeth amounted to that. "May I take it then that you won't feel obliged to stop by every morning to make sure the unfortunate slob next door hasn't accidentally fallen out of bed during the night and broken his miserable neck?''

"You may safely assume exactly that," she said recklessly. "In fact, you may wheel yourself right off the end of the dock and drown, for all I care!"

And grabbing Bounder by the collar again, she'd marched past Liam McGuire and out of his house without so much as a backward glance. Not for the world would she have let him see how rattled she was by his attitude, or how appalled at her own behavior. Only when she reached the cover of the rock behind which she now huddled had she allowed the rigid set of her shoulders to relax and the shame to flood through her.

How *could* she have said such things—she who knew better than most the frustrations and agony of being confined to a wheelchair? Where was the compassion which had come so easily to her when Derek was alive?

It dried up with his death and I will not be drawn into such a web of pain again. I could not survive it a second time.

She closed her eyes, as if doing so would silence the truth echoing through her mind. But one thing she had learned too thoroughly ever to forget: turning away from the facts did nothing to change them. Like it or not, the man next door was disabled. How seriously, she didn't know, but she understood now why the shutters remained in place over the windows, and why he hadn't hung his clothes in the closet.

And with a defeated sigh, she knew that, no matter how unwelcome he might find her visits, sooner or later she'd come knocking on his door again, because she could no more ignore him or his plight than she could turn back the tide creeping up the beach.

"Son of a bitch!"

He slumped in the wheelchair and glared at his hands, clenched into fists in his lap. As if he didn't have enough on his plate without having to contend with a next-door neighbor who had "Good Samaritan" written all over her face!

He'd seen the way she looked, immediately after she'd told him to go drown himself—as if she'd just swallowed a red-hot potato whole!—and he knew what would happen next. The stiff-necked pride which had carried her out of sight along the beach would evaporate faster than that morning's early mist, and be replaced by a great surge of guilt embroidered with pity. She'd belabor herself for having spoken harshly to the gimp in the wheelchair and feel compelled to come back and be kind.

She'd train her big brown eyes on him and stammer out an apology, with a glimmer of penitent tears thrown in for extra effect. Worse, she'd probably bake something in the form of a peace offering—bran muffins most likely, because everyone knew that not getting enough exercise tended to have a detrimental effect on a man's innards.

Swinging the wheelchair around, he rolled out to the front porch again and checked his watch. Almost ten-thirty. She'd been gone nearly half an hour and by now was likely wallowing up to her earlobes in remorse. Give her another hour to slave over a hot stove, and he'd bet money she'd reappear shortly after noon.

And maybe it wouldn't be such a bad thing if she

did. Since he'd run out of fish heads, he could use her bran muffins for crab bait. Shuffling his sorry backside into the runabout and motoring out to the traps was awkward and time-consuming, but worth every ounce of effort for the pleasure he got in feasting on freshly caught rock crab steamed in wine over a bed of coals in the outdoor fire pit.

Good food and wine were among the few pleasures he got from life these days and, under different circumstances, he might have invited her to join him for dinner. If she had a bit more meat on her bones, he'd probably have tried to get her in the sack, as well, because even skinny as a reed, she was a good-looking woman. Decidedly feminine, elegant, and with something fragile about her that, once, would have brought out his protective instincts.

Just as well he was confined to fantasizing about sex these days, though, because she was also the type who'd expect a lot more in return than respect the morning after! When he got on his feet again and was good for something other than swallowing painkillers and feeling sorry for himself, he'd make up for lost playtime but, if he was half as smart as he liked to think he was, it wouldn't be with Jane Ogilvie. Because she was clearly the marrying kind. And he definitely was not.

A movement down on the beach caught his attention. Uh-oh! There she went, right on cue: a woman on a mission if ever he saw one, climbing the sloping path to the house next door with an unmistakable sense of purpose in her step, while her dizzy hound gamboled clumsily at her heels. Talk about the odd couple!

Something about his face felt strange—an odd sort of ache as if he were bringing into play muscles which hadn't seen much use lately—and he realized that, for the second time in less than an hour, he was genuinely amused. He even laughed, though he was so badly out of practice that he sounded like a seal with a bad case of laryngitis.

Well, what the hell! A bit of free entertainment on the side would help pass the time.

Letting a smile settle on his mouth, he leaned forward in the chair and waited for scene two to unfold: Goldilocks on a mission of mercy—except with that mane of dark brown hair, the name Goldilocks didn't exactly suit her.

For the rest of that day and most of the next, Jane turned a deaf ear on the urgings of her guilty conscience. In light of the way Liam McGuire had received her the first time, he was unlikely to welcome another visit anytime soon. It would be best if she gave him time to simmer down before inflicting herself on him again.

But it wasn't easy staying away, and for all that she managed to keep herself busy around her own house, no amount of self-discipline could prevent her from looking out of her bedroom window last thing at night to make sure lamplight showed between the cracks in the shutters on the cottage next door. Or from checking first thing in the morning for the telltale column of smoke that showed he was up and about.

"It's absurd that he's living there alone," she complained to Bounder. "In fact, it's unconscionable. He has no right burdening total strangers with responsibility for his welfare."

But that line of reasoning soon fell by the wayside and it was all the fault of those darned shutters.

Well...theirs and the heat wave which struck out of nowhere two days later and showed signs of staying awhile. How, after all, could any woman with an ounce of charity to her name ignore the fact that, with temperatures suddenly soaring to the mid-eighties, Steve's place, boarded up as it was, would be like an oven by the end of the day?

So, armed with a small crowbar and a hammer, she set off after breakfast on the third morning, determined that nothing Liam McGuire could fling at her in the way of insults would provoke her into leaving before she'd accomplished the task she'd set herself.

Once again, she found his front door open, propped wide this time with an old flat iron acting as a stop, and she could see that he'd made some attempt to clean up the kitchen. A plate, two coffee mugs, a frying pan and a handful of cutlery were stacked neatly in a dish rack next to the sink, and he'd spread a tea towel over the porch railing to dry.

She'd learned her lesson, though, and didn't repeat the mistake of walking in when he didn't respond to her polite knock. With both feet planted on the porch, she leaned forward and gave the door a mighty thump with her hammer. "Are you there, Mr. McGuire? It's Jane Ogilvie from next door."

Still no reply, nor any movement but Steve's old hammock strung from the porch rafters and swinging in the hot breeze. Assuming Liam McGuire wasn't deaf or dead, he must be out again, though where he went, given his condition and the uneven terrain around the cottage, was a mystery not hers to solve.

To do what had to be done, all she needed was the ladder Steve kept in his woodshed, and in all honesty, she was just as glad not to have an audience. Carpentry, even the crude kind she was about to tackle, had never been her forte. She could very well do without the sarcastic running commentary Liam McGuire would no doubt have offered, had he been there to witness her efforts as she wrestled the boards away from the windows and stored them under the porch where they normally spent the summer.

Things went well enough to begin with, though having to move the ladder every few yards used up an astonishing amount of energy, but the real trouble began when she tackled the bedroom windows. All the others opened onto the porch which offered a nice stable platform from which to work. The ground below the bedroom, however, fell away steeply and was knee-deep in grass, stinging nettles and wild honeysuckle.

Doubtfully, she sized up the situation. Finding a firm footing for the ladder was difficult enough, but scaling rungs fully fifteen feet in the air taxed her dwindling courage to the limit. She'd never had a good head for heights. And to make matters worse, the glare from the sun hitting the uncovered glass half blinded her.

"Careful, Bounder!" she exclaimed at one point, clinging to the window frame as he charged past and headed up the slope toward the house with more than usual exuberance. "Up-end this ladder while I'm on it and you and I are going to have a very serious falling out."

From somewhere on the deck, Liam McGuire's sardonic tones floated back a reply. "That's assuming you live to talk about it, Goldilocks. In case you didn't notice, your dumb dog just disturbed a wasps' nest and unless you want to risk being badly stung, you're going to have to stay where you are until it gets dark which, by my reckoning, isn't going to happen for another eleven hours.''

Given his sour disposition, there was every chance he was lying, just to provoke her. But the buzzing sound which she'd vaguely noticed and attributed to the electric generator gave undeniable credence to his words. "When did you get back?" she said, suddenly and deeply regretting having yielded to the whim to do him a favor.

"More to the point, when did you?" he said. "I don't recall inviting you, though I do distinctly remember your assuring me you wouldn't bother me again."

The buzzing grew ominously closer and she cringed, certain that at any minute she'd feel insect feet crawling up her bare legs. "Do you think," she said, hanging on by her fingernails, "that we could pursue this discussion *after* I've figured a way out of my present predicament?"

"You?" He gave a bark of contemptuous laughter. "You couldn't figure your way out of a brown paper bag without help. Face it, honey, you're the one needing favors from *me*, this time—unless you think Blunder's about to come to the rescue."

"His name's Bounder," she said from between clenched teeth. "And if it's all the same to you, I'd appreciate it if you'd try to keep him away from the foot of this ladder. I don't want him to get stung."

"Well, heaven forfend!" He was jeering at her again but, to his credit, he snapped his fingers sharply and, in quite a different voice, ordered, "Blunder, come!"

Amazingly, she heard the faint click of claws on the wooden porch, followed by a thump as Liam McGuire rapped out, "Sit!"

"Pity you don't have an equally winning way with people," she couldn't help observing.

"I'd save the smart-ass remarks until I was safely on firm ground again, if I were you," he said. "You're in no position to be passing judgment on anyone, least of all the guy you expect to come to your rescue."

She ventured a look down and hastily closed her eyes as the ground swam up to meet her. "How are you going to get me down, with all those wasps swarming around?"

"I'm not," he said. "And if that's what you're hoping for, you're in for a disappointment. Your only choice is to haul the rest of the boards off that window which I'll then open from the inside so you can crawl through."

Swing one leg over that narrow sill? Heavenly days, it was all she could do to maintain her balance with both feet planted on the ladder rung! "I...don't think I can do that, Mr. McGuire."

"Then I hope you remembered to go pee before you came over here, because you're stuck up there for the duration," he said bluntly.

Oh, he was the most vulgar, insensitive man ever to walk the face of the earth and, forgetting to be cautious, she swung her head around to tell him so. But the ladder gave a shudder, as though to remind her that it wouldn't take much to send it—and her—sliding down the slope.

"All right, we'll do it your way," she said faintly.

"Good girl."

Was it possible that was a hint of sympathy—of kindness even, that she heard in his voice?

"Stay put until I get myself into the bedroom," he went on. "Then do exactly as I tell you."

The wheelchair whispered away and a moment later his voice came again, this time on the other side of the shutters. "This is your lucky day, Janie. The window slides open so all you need to do is pry off a couple of boards and make an opening wide enough to get your butt through. I'll take care of the rest."

She had no reason to believe him, at least on the last point. Not only was he wheelchair-bound, he'd shown no inclination to be chivalrous. Yet what choice did she have but to put herself at his mercy?

"Well?" he asked, impatience already eroding his temporary show of kindness. "Make up your mind. Do we have a deal or not?"

"We have a deal," she said. "Thank you, Mr. McGuire."

CHAPTER TWO

How he managed it, she didn't know—nor, given her precarious situation, did Jane choose that moment to demand any explanations. It was enough that one minute she was teetering in midair, almost afraid to breathe as she wrestled the first board loose, and the next, he'd reached through six inches of open window to bring the whole operation to a speedy conclusion.

That solidly muscular forearm and the unshakeable strength in his hand reassured her as nothing else could. In no time, the rest of the glass was uncovered. All that remained was for her to gather up what was left of her courage and climb inside the house.

It should have been easy; would have been, if she hadn't immediately realized that the ladder was positioned too far to the left of the open end of the window. A full two feet of empty space separated her from safety, and the mere idea of launching herself across it was as far-fetched as trying to leap the Grand Canyon.

Liam McGuire saw her hesitation. "You haven't come this far to chicken out now," he said. "Quit scaring yourself witless and get on with it."

Perspiration prickled all over her body.

Perspiration, nothing! It was sweat, pure and simple, imprisoning her in clammy fear. "I can't do it," she quavered, eyeing the chasm between them.

"You can't *not* do it, woman!" he said flatly. "You got yourself into this mess and since I'm damn near useless in this wheelchair, you're going to have to get yourself out. So stop the hyperventilating, grab a hold of the top of the window frame, and climb onto the ledge. There's nothing to it.''

Nothing to it? Her voice rose nearly a full octave. "Are you out of your mind? That ledge is scarcely wide enough to hold a seagull!''

He glared at her from eyes turned brilliant aquamarine in the reflection of sunlight on water. It was the kind of look which, all by itself, probably had subordinates leaping to obey his every command, but when all she did was stare back in frozen terror, he lost his temper and bellowed, "Oh, for crying out loud! Just what the doctor ordered for a full and speedy recovery—a hundred and fifteen pounds of catatonic woman perched on a ladder twenty feet in the air, and expecting Superman to fly to the rescue!''

Letting go of her hand, he abruptly disappeared from view and, for one horrified moment, she thought he was going to resolve matters by abandoning her to the wasps and stinging nettles down below. From somewhere inside the room she heard a shuffling and a string of curses that, even in her panic-stricken state, left the tips of her ears burning.

Then, just as abruptly, he reappeared, except this time there was more of him to see than just his head and shoulders. The entire upper half of his body was visible, too.

"Okay," he said. "Let's try this again.''

"No," she said. "I can't. I'm too scared.''

"I'll be nice to your dog if you don't chicken out on me," he wheedled in what she supposed he considered to be his most winning way. "I won't use him for target practice the next time I feel like shooting the pellet gun Coffey keeps under the bed. I won't even tell anyone that I caught you messing around with my underpants.''

What he no doubt perceived to be irresistible bribes struck her as nothing short of blackmail. "You're a horrible man,'' she whimpered.

He wasn't one to tolerate having his suggestions thwarted. "What the devil is it you want of me?'' he roared, immediately reverting to his usual confrontational self. "A pint of blood? A pound of flesh? I can't maintain this position indefinitely, you know!''

Only then did it fully sink in that he'd hauled himself out of the chair and was propping himself upright by taking all his weight on one arm, while he reached out to her with the other.

The sweat pearling his face attested to what the effort was costing him and shamed her out of her own cowardice. "All right, you win,'' she said faintly and quickly, before the foolhardiness of the undertaking had time to impress itself on her brain, she crabbed one foot onto the ledge and literally hurled herself at him.

Her knuckles and knees scraped against the cedar shingles and she managed to clip the side of her head on the ladder in passing, but the pain scarcely registered beside the utter relief of feeling him grasp a fistful of the front of her T-shirt and yank her the rest of the way to safety.

"Aah!'' she gasped, landing in a winded heap at his feet. "Thank you *so* much! I owe you big-time for this.''

He expelled a mighty breath, literally falling like a sack of potatoes into the wheelchair, and swung it toward the living room. "Oh, please, no! The last thing I need is any more of your favors. You're more trouble than you're worth.''

"It wouldn't hurt you to show a bit of gratitude, as well, you know," she said, picking herself up and trailing after him. "Most people would be happy to have windows they could open, rather than live in a place as dark as a cave."

"In case you haven't noticed, Goldilocks, I'm not 'most people.' If I were, I'd have taken care of the problem myself, instead of having to fall back on the services of a semi-competent woman with a bad case of acrophobia." He positioned himself in front of one of the lower kitchen cabinets and hauled out a bottle of Scotch. "I could use a drink and so, I imagine, could you."

"At this hour of the morning?" she protested. "I hardly think—"

"And you can spare me your homilies on the evils of booze, as well! I'll get plastered any time I feel like it, and right now, I feel like it."

She opened her mouth to tell him that drowning his sorrows in alcohol wouldn't make them go away, then thought better of it when she saw that a grayish pallor undermined the deep tan of his face. Even his hand shook as he unscrewed the cap on the bottle.

Moved by a compassion that had its roots in another time when she'd been equally helpless to alleviate suffering, she covered his hand with hers and took the bottle away. "Let me," she said quietly, and splashed a scant half inch of whiskey into a glass.

He tossed it down in one gulp, cradled the glass in his hands, then leaned back in the chair with his eyes closed. He had a rather wonderful face, even with that devastatingly direct gaze hidden, she decided, taking advantage of the chance to study him unobserved; a face that revealed far more about the man who owned it than he probably realized.

She saw strength in the line of his jaw, laughter in the fan of lines beside his eyes, passion and discipline in the curve of his mouth. His recent proclamation notwithstanding, he was no drinker. He showed too much pride for such self-indulgence.

"You can leave anytime," he said, not moving a muscle more than was needed to spit out the words. "I'm not going to do the socially acceptable thing and invite you to stay for coffee."

"Then I'll invite myself," she said, and without waiting for permission, filled the kettle and set it to boil on the stove. "How do you take yours?"

"Alone, thank you very much."

She shrugged and inspected the contents of the refrigerator. Beyond a block of cheese, a couple of eggs, an open carton of milk, some bread and the remains of something which, under the layer of green mold, might have been meat, the shelves were empty.

She sniffed the milk and immediately wished she hadn't. "This milk went off about a week ago, Mr. McGuire."

"I know," he said, a current of unholy mirth running through his voice, and when she turned back to face him, she saw he was observing her with malicious glee. "I saved it on purpose, just for the pleasure of seeing your expression when you stuck your interfering nose into yet another part of my life. Would you like to taste the ham, as well, while you're at it?"

She emptied the milk down the sink drain and tossed the ham into the garbage can. "Whoever does your shopping is falling down on the job, but since I'm planning on going across to Clara's Cove later on today, I can stop by the general store and pick up a few staples for you, if you like.''

"What is it you don't understand about 'Mind Your Own Business'?'' The question ricocheted off the walls like machine gun bullets. "What do I have to do to make it clear that I'm perfectly able to shop for myself? How do I let you know that you can take your charity and shove it, because *I neither want it nor need it?*''

She recognized the insults for what they really were: bitter resentment at only recently finding himself confined to a wheelchair. When the same thing had first happened to Derek, he'd reacted much the same way and it had taken months for him to come to terms with how his life was going to be from then on.

"I know how difficult you must find all this, Mr. McGuire,'' she said, "and I certainly didn't mean to offend you.''

"Unless you've been where I am now, you don't know beans about how I feel!''

She washed and rinsed the plate which had held the ham, placed it in the dish rack, and made the coffee. "Actually, I do,'' she said. "My husband—''

"Oh, goodie, you have a husband, you have a husband!'' he gibed. "That being the case, why don't you run along and minister to him, instead of foisting your attentions on me?''

"Because he's dead,'' she said baldly.

Shock, and perhaps even a little shame, wiped the sneer off Liam McGuire's face. "Oh, cripes,'' he muttered, examining his hands. "I'm sorry. That must be tough. You're kind of young to be a widow.''

She dried her scraped knuckles tenderly, folded the dish towel over the edge of the counter, and turned to leave. "I'm not looking for your sympathy, any more than you're looking for mine, Mr. McGuire. But take it from me, people can and do adapt—if they've a mind to. Of course, if all they're interested in is wallowing in self-pity, they can do that, too, though why they'd find it an attractive alternative baffles me since it must be a very lonely occupation. Good day.''

"Hey!"

She was almost at the door when he stopped her. "You called?" she inquired sweetly, not bothering to turn around.

"Are you by any chance a schoolteacher?"

"Not that it's any of your business, but no. Why do you ask?"

"Because you talk like one."

"I see. Is there anything else, Mr. McGuire?"

"Yes," he said irritably. "You can stop calling me Mister McGuire in that snotty way. My name's Liam."

"How nice! Will that be all, Liam?"

He thumped the flat of one hand on the armrest of his chair and rolled his eyes toward the ceiling as though calling on divine intervention to save him from himself. "I'm going to regret this later," he announced morosely, then swung his gaze back to her. "Since you've made the damn coffee anyway, you might as well stay and have a cup. There's canned milk in the cupboard, if you want it."

"That's very kind of you, I'm sure, but I just remembered that Bounder's outside and I don't want him running loose all over the island."

"Bring the benighted hound inside, then. It won't be the first time he's made himself at home here."

"My goodness!" she said, unable to quell the mean-spirited pleasure of having finally wrung a concession from him. "How can I refuse such a gracious offer?"

He waited until the coffee was served, she had taken a seat on the couch, and Bounder was snoozing beside the wheelchair, before he spoke again. "Have you been...by yourself for very long?"

"Just over two years."

He stared into his mug. "What you said, about understanding how I feel in this chair, was your husband...?"

"Yes, for the better part of the last three years of his life."

He averted his gaze, but not before she saw the grimace he couldn't control. "I'd go mad if I was facing that length of time," he said.

"It's amazing what people come to accept when they don't have any other choices."

"Not me," he said. "I'm not handing over control of my life to anything or anyone else, especially not a bunch of doctors who don't know what they're talking about. According to them, I should settle for being alive with both legs still attached, and never mind expecting to walk again. But I'll show them! It'll take more structural failure at the bottom of an offshore oil rig to keep me tied to a wheelchair for the rest of my life."

Good grief, the man lived dangerously! She'd seen news reports and documentaries about offshore drilling for oil. The rigs had struck her as frighteningly inhospitable, even those parts above the water. She couldn't imagine how much worse they'd be fathoms deep in the ocean. "I gather," she said, treading delicately, "that you had an accident of some kind?"

"You could put it like that, yeah. I found myself pinned under a steel beam and had a bit of trouble getting free."

Since he was so determined to dismiss what had clearly been a life-threatening incident as something of no great consequence, she deemed it wise to respond in like fashion. Tilting one shoulder in a faint shrug, she said, "Well, there's no doubt that, given the will and a reasonable amount of luck, some people do make remarkable recoveries. May I pour you more coffee before I leave?"

"You're leaving already? Why? Where's the fire?"

If he hadn't already gone to such lengths to try to get rid of her, she'd have thought he wanted her to stay a bit longer. But, *Wishful thinking, Jane,* she told herself. *You're just dazzled by those beautiful sea-green eyes.*

"No fire," she said, as much to refute her own foolishness as to answer his remark. "Just the opposite, in fact. I want to take Bounder down for a swim before the tide turns."

At the mention of his name, the dog reared up in excitement, a running shoe clamped in his mouth.

"He needs a few lessons in obedience, if you ask me," Liam said, grabbing the shoe and flinging it under the table, then seizing his coffee cup before it was swept on the floor by Bounder's thrashing tail. "He's out of control. Settle down, idiot!"

"He's not much more than a puppy," Jane said defensively. "He's still learning and I have to be patient."

"Patient, my eye! He's already mastered one lesson and that's how to control you! If you were as dedicated to making him behave and keeping his teeth off other people's property, as you are to nosing around in business that doesn't concern you, you'd be a sight better

off and so would he. He's too damned big to be ga-
lumphing around like this.''

She swallowed a laugh. ''Well, the truce was nice
while it lasted, but it's clearly over so I'll get us both
out of your hair before you start tearing it out by the
roots. Thanks for the coffee. Come on, Bounder.''

''Yeah, well…thanks. For what you did. With the
shutters, and all.''

He might have been having all his teeth pulled without benefit of anesthetic, he sounded so pained! But
she made allowances because she knew that his pride
was injured at least as badly as his leg. Anyone could
see that Liam McGuire wasn't accustomed to being
helpless and that it particularly went against the grain
for him to have to watch a woman take on what he
considered to be a man's job.

''You're welcome,'' she said. ''Thanks for rescuing
me.''

''It's the only way I could think of to get rid of
you.''

The smile which accompanied his remark, though
meager, transformed his face. Charmed more than she
cared to admit, Jane smiled back and said, ''I'll make
a deal with you. I promise not to bother you again,
provided you agree to call on me if you need help.''

''And how do you propose I do that, Goldilocks?''

''Tie a towel or something to the post at the end of
the porch railing so I can see it from my place.''

He chewed the corner of his lip thoughtfully, then
shrugged and extended his hand. ''Sounds like a one-
sided deal to me, but if that's what it'll take to keep
the peace.…''

Since he'd shown a near-aversion to touching her
any more than was absolutely necessary, she expected

his handshake would be brief and businesslike. But, noticing her raw knuckles, he stroked his thumb carefully across her fingers and said, "You've chewed yourself up pretty badly. Do you have something you can put on these to prevent infection?"

"Yes." His concern, though impersonal, left her foolishly misty-eyed.

He noticed that, too. Misinterpreting the reason for her distress, he said, "Are they hurting that badly, Jane?"

"Uh-uh." She swallowed and shook her head. "It's just that I'm not used to having someone be concerned about me. It's usually the other way around."

Raising his eyes, he subjected her to a brief, intense scrutiny before dropping her hand and turning the wheelchair toward the door. "Then go put some salve on your scrapes and look after yourself for a change. You've wasted enough time on me for one day."

She felt his gaze following her all the way along the path. Before climbing the steps to her own front porch, she looked back and sure enough, he'd stationed himself beside the post at the edge of the porch. When he saw her turn, he lifted his hand in a salute. She did the same and, fanciful though it might be, it was as if a small flame sprang alive in the cold, empty wasteland which for so long had been her heart.

That simple gesture set the pattern for the days which followed. Whenever they happened to see one another from a distance, they'd mark the occasion with a wave, an acknowledgment which, though wordless, nevertheless conveyed a sense of cautious awareness of each other.

Once, she saw him seated at the wheel of Steve's

eighteen-foot runabout and heading across the stretch
of water separating Bell Island from Clara's Cove on
Regis Island. Another time she caught sight of him
hauling driftwood up the ramp from the beach. But
though her every instinct screamed for her to go over
and make sure he was coping by himself, she honored
their pact and kept her distance.

The heat wave softened to the more typically tem-
perate warmth of early July, with cool, refreshing
nights and mornings cloaked in milky haze. The leisurely days worked their magic and Jane found the
healing, the sense of contentment and peace within herself, which had for so long evaded her.

She spent evenings sitting on the porch in one of the
wooden Adirondack chairs her grandfather had made
years before, and watching the first stars come out.
Early each morning she left a trail of footprints along
the newly-washed sand at the water's edge. She swam
in the sun-warmed waters of the cove, and hiked the
lower slopes of Bell Mountain to pick wild blueberries.
She taught Bounder to sit and stay on command.

Her skin took on a sun glow and she gained a pound
or two because her arms and legs no longer seemed
quite so scrawny. She slept like a child—deeply,
dreamlessly—and rediscovered a serenity of spirit
she'd thought she'd lost forever.

Sometimes, she thought she could live like that indefinitely, hidden away with only Bounder for company and the bald eagles and killer whales to witness
her comings and goings. But nothing stayed the same
for very long. Time, life—they moved forward. Change
occurred.

For her, it began the morning she went outside and
found a pail of fresh clams at the foot of her porch

steps. He didn't bother leaving a note, but she knew Liam had to be the one who'd left them there, though how he'd found the stamina to navigate the rutted path from his place to hers she couldn't begin to fathom.

In return, she waited until she saw him take the boat from its mooring, then sneaked over and left a loaf of freshly baked bread outside his door.

And so they established another tenuous line of communication: half a small salmon from him, a bowl of wild strawberries from her; apple pie still warm from her oven as thanks for prawns the size of small lobsters which he hauled out of the deep water of the mid-channel. And all done furtively so as not to contravene the terms of their pact of peaceful but independent co-existence.

Then, one time, she noticed his unoccupied wheelchair leaning drunkenly against the post at the top of the ramp leading to the house. Afraid that he'd somehow lost control of it, she sneaked over and crept up the ramp to his cottage, dreading what she might discover.

She found him stationed on the seaward side of the porch. Using the railing for support, he was testing his weight on his injured leg.

Be careful! You can't rush recovery! she wanted to cry out, because he was a big man, tall and powerfully built. And the fact that he was trembling with the effort it cost him to put himself through the exercise told her he was pushing himself too hard, too soon.

Her concern wasn't entirely altruistic. She knew a tiny disappointment, too, because as his recovery progressed, the likelihood that he'd call on her for help grew increasingly remote. And solitude, she was beginning to learn, had its drawbacks. There was only so much intelligent conversation one could hold with a dog, even one as smart as Bounder.

Apparently, Liam McGuire reached the same conclusion because a few days later, instead of leaving an offering of food, he left a note.

You can come for dinner tonight, if you want to, and bring the dog. Seven o'clock.

Not the most gracious invitation, perhaps, but a gilt-engraved summons issued by royalty could not have thrilled her more. "See you at seven," she scribbled back, anchored the reply under a rock on his porch railing, and, in a fever of anticipation, rushed home to make wild raspberry tart.

While it baked, she hauled the big tin bath tub in from the back porch to the middle of the kitchen floor, filled it with water heated in a pail on the stove, and soaked luxuriously. She shampooed the sea salt out of her hair, then rinsed it in cool water from the rain barrel outside. She creamed perfumed lotion all over her sun-dried skin and fished out the meager supply of cosmetics which hadn't seen the light of day since she'd arrived on the island. She ironed one of the few dresses she'd brought with her, a sleeveless, delphinium blue cotton affair with a full skirt and fitted waist.

After all that, when seven o'clock rolled around, she knew the most frightful attack of nerves, wiped the lipstick off her mouth, threw the dress to the back of the closet, and put on a clean pair of red shorts and a matching top.

"As if it matters what I wear," she told Bounder. "I could show up stark naked and he probably wouldn't care, as long as I don't presume too much on his hospitality.''

He'd acted against his better judgment and was living to regret it. Had regretted it, if truth be known, ever since he'd slunk away from her front step after leaving the note. Cabin fever must have taken hold without his realizing it. Why else would he deliberately sabotage his well-ordered life by inviting her and her demented dog to intrude on it? And why would he waste the better of the afternoon trying to tart the place up to look more than it really was? The picnic table on the grass below the porch had seen better days, and paper towels hardly qualified as fine linen.

He poured himself a glass of wine from the ice chest at his side and wheeled himself over to the railing overlooking the beach. It was almost a quarter after seven and she struck him as the punctual type, so the odds were she'd changed her mind about joining him for dinner, which was fine by him. It wasn't as if her share of the food would go to waste. The energy it had taken for him to organize the meal had left him ravenous.

Funny thing, though, how a man's mood could shift. That afternoon, while he'd readied the outdoor fire pit for action, he'd found himself whistling under his breath. He'd believed he was looking forward to the evening, to watching her face break into a smile, to hearing her laughter.

After a while, a guy got sick of the sound of his own voice, and sicker still of the same old thoughts chasing around inside his head. *Was he ever going to walk under his own steam again? Was he finished as the expert everyone called on to design a new offshore project?*

He needed distraction and under normal circum-

stances, he'd have found it with other people. With
women—though not with a particular woman because
that usually led to complications.

No, Jane Ogilvie had done him a favor by canceling
out, no doubt about it. Start feeding her, and she'd be
moving in before he had time to bolt the door. She had
a thoroughly domesticated look about her, and if proof
was what he needed to back up the opinion, she'd provided it with all that home baking. So what if she'd
never actually produced bran muffins? She managed to
make just about everything else, which amounted to
the same thing.

He took another swig of the wine and rubbed his
newly shaven jaw irritably. Scraping off several days'
growth of beard had left his skin tender as a newborn
baby's backside—and that was all her fault, too. If she
hadn't moved in next door, he'd have remained a contented, unkempt slob of a hermit, instead of jumping
through hoops trying to make himself look half decent
when the only facilities at his disposal were a cold-
water shower and a pint-size mirror hanging over the
kitchen sink.

From the corner of his eye, he caught a movement
to the left of the porch, a flutter of red and a blur of
black, followed shortly thereafter by the thud of paws
galloping up the wooden ramp to the porch, and the
unmistakable whiff of ripe berries.

To counteract the completely absurd rush of satisfaction threatening to wipe out his ill humor, he shuf-
fled lower in the wheelchair and glowered determinedly
at the sun sliding down in the west. Why the devil
couldn't she have stayed at home where she belonged?

CHAPTER THREE

"SORRY we're late," she said, balancing the raspberry tart on one hand and trying to control Bounder with the other.

"I didn't notice you were," Liam said, apparently too mesmerized by the ribbons of lavender and rose strung across the western horizon to notice the time, let alone her. "Is it seven already?"

"Almost half past, actually. I was afraid you'd have given up on me."

"The thought never crossed my mind." Rousing himself to a less supine position, he inspected the contents of his glass and said sullenly, "I was too busy enjoying my solitude."

So it was to be like that, was it? Pressing her lips together in annoyance, Jane gave silent thanks to whatever minor god had urged her not to overdress for her role in what promised to be nothing short of a dinner farce. "I hope my coming here hasn't put you out too much."

"Not a bit. We've both got to eat, and it's not as if we plan to make a habit of joining forces." He slewed a glance her way and gave an exaggerated start of surprise at the sight of the tart. "Oh, gee, you baked a pie! Why doesn't that surprise me? Stick it in the cooler over there, why don't you? And while you're at it, pour yourself a glass of wine. I'd get up and do the honors myself but—"

"Oh, please! I wouldn't dream of expecting you to bestir yourself."

37

Obtuse as he was, even he caught the edge in her tone. "Exactly what *are* you expecting, Jane? That I'm going to treat you as if you're a date? Because if so, you're in for a disappointment. I happened to catch enough crab for two and since you're my nearest neighbor, I invited you to share the feast. The fact that you're reasonably young and not too ugly has no relevance. I'd have done the same if you'd been seventy-nine and toothless."

"I'm more relieved to hear that than you can possibly begin to guess," she cooed, the "not too ugly" label stinging worse than anything a wasp could inflict. "Because, loath though I am to damage your massive ego, if a date *had* been what you had in mind, I'd have been obliged to turn you down. You're not my kind of man."

"And what kind of man is that?" he asked offhandedly. "Someone with two good legs who can chase you all over the island, then throw you over his shoulder and carry you off to his lair to have his wicked way with you?"

"No," she said shortly. "But a working brain is a definite must and yours, I begin to suspect, has yet to be taken out of the box it came in."

Her observation caught him squarely as he drained his glass, turning the chuckle he couldn't quite smother into a coughing fit as the wine went down the wrong way. "Okay," he croaked, when at last he managed to regain his breath, "you win this round. I admit I was ticked off when it seemed you were a no-show and I acted like an idiot. Can we start over, if I promise to polish my skills as a host?"

"I'm not sure," she said, even though trying to hang on to her annoyance in the face of such a disarming confession was a lost cause, particularly with Bounder fawning shamelessly all over the object of her displeasure. "I can't say I was flattered by your description of me."

Steering his chair around the hammock to where Steve's old kerosene storm lantern sat on a shelf on the wall, Liam put a match to the wick. Just briefly, before he swung around to face her again, the aura of light limned his features in gold and revealed the smile lurking at the corner of his mouth. "You mean the bit about your being not bad-looking?"

"That's not quite how you worded it, but since we're aiming for a fresh start, I won't quibble over semantics."

"In that case," he said, heading down the ramp to the grassy area below, "if you wouldn't mind pouring the wine, I'll get the fire started, and we can engage in idle gossip and watch the sun go down while we wait for the water to boil."

Somehow, she doubted Liam McGuire was the kind of man who ever wasted time being idle about anything. He was too full of a restless energy turned inward by the physical restrictions he was forced to endure. Talk about an inquiring mind! He didn't just look at a person, he looked inside her, his cool gaze probing her most private thoughts.

She'd no sooner joined him at the fire pit than the inquisition began. "Cheers," he said, raising his glass to hers, and before she had time to acknowledge the toast, let alone take a sip of the wine, went on, "Tell me how your better half wound up in a wheelchair."

"*What?*" She stared at him in offended disbelief. Was the man completely insensitive to everyone's pain but his own?

"Tell me about your husband. I'm curious."

"Well, that's certainly stating the obvious! The question is, why do you want to know?"

"Well, we've got to talk about something and the last time you were here, you made some remark about understanding my frustration at being in this damned contraption because you'd seen him go through the same thing." He shrugged, and poked at a chunk of driftwood which had fallen away from the flames. "But if talking about it touches a nerve, we can always debate the vanishing ozone layer or the migration of the otter flea."

"I didn't know otters had fleas," she said stiffly.

Leaning toward her, he planted his elbow on the arm of his chair, rested his chin on his fist, and fixed her in that disturbing gaze of his. "His death's still too painful to talk about, huh, even after two years?"

"It'll never be easy. But I've come to terms with it."

"What went wrong? An accident of some sort?"

"No. He had ALS. Amyotrophic lateral sclerosis, although most people call it—"

"Lou Gehrig's disease." He grimaced. "Yeah, I know. It's one of those things that…well, I don't have to tell you. You lived it. How long was your husband…?"

"Seven years. We'd been married only eighteen months when he was diagnosed."

Liam inhaled sharply. "Barely past the honeymoon stage! You can't have been much more than a kid. And you hung in over the long haul?"

"Well, of course I did!" she said indignantly. "What did you think? That I'd walk out on him because he didn't remain the perfect, healthy specimen I'd married?''

"A lot of women would have, wedding vows about sticking it out in sickness and in health notwithstanding.''

"If you believe that, then you obviously don't know much about love.''

"Maybe not, but I know a lot about women.''

Jane stared at him, taken aback by the surge of bitterness which colored his remark, and suddenly as curious about his past as he was about hers. "I don't suppose you'd care to elaborate on that?''

"Not particularly.'' Awkwardly, he bent to wedge another piece of wood under Steve's old metal crab pot. She could have done it for him in a fraction of the time, but she knew better than to offer.

"It's going to take a while for this water to come to a boil,'' Liam said, "but I've got nuts and stuff to snack on while we're waiting. If you want to make yourself useful, you could get them—they're in the kitchen—and bring another bottle of wine out of the refrigerator.''

He'd tidied the place up in her honor she noticed when she went inside. The floor had been swept and the counter was empty except for a cardboard box holding cutlery, plates and a roll of paper towels, a loaf of bread, a bag of prepared salad greens, and some packages of nuts and pretzels.

She found the wine and a corkscrew, and emptied the snacks into a wooden salad bowl. When she went back outside, the fire had taken hold and Liam sat with his gaze fixed moodily on the flames licking up the side of the blackened old pot, and Bounder sleeping next to his chair.

Taking a seat at the picnic table, Jane helped herself
to a handful of nuts before passing the bowl to Liam.
He nodded his thanks and for a while nothing disturbed
the silence except the occasional cry of a seagull and
the spit and crackle of the driftwood fire. The sky had
paled to winter melon green with the sun's passing and
the first faint stars twinkled to the east.

From where she sat, Jane was able to take in the
sweep of ocean and distant mountains and, much closer
at hand, her host's unruly mop of dark hair and width
of shoulder.

*What happened to make you so wary of other peo-
ple?* she longed to ask, and knew a shocking urge to
reach out and touch him. There was such a loneliness
about his still figure, such a need for gentleness.

Suddenly, as if he knew she was burning up with
curiosity, he announced, "You aren't the only one
who's been married, you know. I tried it once myself."

He flung the information down like a challenge, as
if daring her to take issue with it. "Did you?" she said
mildly.

When he didn't immediately reply, she left it at that
and for a while the silence came swarming back, seem-
ing deeper with encroaching night. The flames grew
brighter, higher, and a mist of steam rose from the crab
pot. Bounder stirred and shifted to a more comfortable
position, with his nose nudging the wheelchair's foot-
rest.

"I'm divorced, in case you're wondering."

In light of his caustic tone of voice, she'd have had
to be mentally defective not to have figured that much
out for herself. But it seemed politic not to say so, so
she stuck to a sympathetic, "I'm sorry."

"I'm not!" His shoulders jerked in bitter amusement. "I consider myself lucky to be rid of her."

"Don't you find that rather sad?"

He tossed her an incredulous glance. "Hell, no! Why should I?"

"Because presumably you were in love with each other once, and when those feelings died, you lost something precious."

"I lost a money-hungry parasite, sweetheart! Caroline kept a calculator where her heart was supposed to be. Her chief hobby was adding up how much a man was worth, and whether he could afford her or not. Love wasn't part of the equation."

"In that case, why did you get married in the first place?"

"I asked myself the same question for years and never did come up with an answer that made any sense. Put it down to a combination of lust, wilful blindness on my part, and great acting on hers. Around the time I found out she wasn't what she'd first seemed, she decided she didn't like the demands of my job and found comfort in some other guy's arms while I was away on a project. Last I heard, she'd dumped *him* for somebody with a fatter wallet."

"I can't imagine any wife behaving like that," Jane said, wondering if his abrasive front was really nothing more than camouflage to hide a broken heart.

"Oh, trust me, it happens! Just because you spent all your free time polishing your halo, don't assume every other woman does the same."

"I resent that," she said, the surge of compassion he'd awoken in her evaporating just as rapidly as it had arisen. "There was nothing long-suffering about my devotion to Derek. I loved him and he loved me, and we both honored our wedding vows. So don't *you* assume just because *your* marriage fell apart, that mine was held together by baling wire and pity, because it wasn't! It was strong enough to stand on its own merits, regardless of what life threw at it.''

"And it ended before the strain began to tell."

"Why, you…you…unfeeling brute!"

"That's me, all right," he said, supremely unmoved by her distress. "Stroking fragile egos isn't one of my talents. I prefer to deal with reality."

"Oh, who do you think you're kidding?" she snorted. "You're so busy trying to ignore the fact that you're handicapped that you can't even accept a little help without getting all bent out of shape. You could give lessons on stroking the fragile ego, as long as it's yours that's getting stroked!"

He bent to scratch Bounder's ear and she heard the laughter in his voice when he said, "That's women for you, Blunder, old pal! Going straight for the jugular. Take my advice and steer clear of the lot of them."

Bounder reared up, placed a paw on Liam's lap, and gazed at him adoringly. Talk about male bonding! The whole performance was enough to turn Jane's stomach. "I'm beginning to wonder why I ever agreed to come here this evening," she said.

Liam gave another of those annoyingly self-satisfied chortles, as though, having his vented his disillusionment with women in general, he could now afford to take a warped kind of pleasure in her company. "Well, it's too late to back out now, sweetheart. The water's boiling and the crabs need to be thrown in the pot."

"I'd offer to help," she said sourly, "but I'm afraid I might give in to the urge to shove you in, as well."

He laughed outright at that, and rolled the wheelchair

dangerously close to the fire. "Watch it, Janie! Your halo's slipping—though I have to admit, I like you better this way. Keep it up and you just might get asked back again. In fact, if things were different, I might have tried to put the moves on you."

His arrogance, she decided balefully, was exceeded only by her foolishness. She had no business feeling all warm and fuzzy inside at his backhanded compliment, and no business at all wondering what it would take to change his views on love and marriage. He was a confirmed bachelor, and just as well because he'd make a lousy husband. Not that she was interested in finding one. She was perfectly content to be remain single, despite what her friends thought.

Two years is long enough to put the grieving behind you and get on with your life, Jane, they'd scolded kindly, and she'd have agreed with them if it weren't for the fact that, to them, "getting on" with her life meant finding a new man. They hadn't understood that she needed time for herself.

"In case you didn't realize, I just paid you a compliment," Liam said, flinging the last of the crabs into the pot. "So why the grim expression?"

"I was thinking."

"If it's that much of an effort, perhaps you shouldn't bother."

She rolled her eyes. "Very funny, I'm sure. Do you ever get through a conversation without slinging a few insults around?"

"Lighten up, Janie. I was just kidding." He watched her narrowly through the swirls of steam rising from the pot. "What dire thoughts took hold so suddenly?"

"I was thinking about my friends. In their opinion, it's time I got married again."

"Cripes, I hope you're not checking me out as a prospective candidate!"

"Don't flatter yourself, McGuire. The reason I came to the island was to get away from all that well-intentioned advice. And even if I felt inclined to follow it, yours would be the last name on the list."

"That's a relief." He stirred the contents of the pot with a long-handled rake, then said, "I thought you claimed yours was a good marriage."

"It was."

"So why the reluctance to get involved again?"

"I'm not saying I plan to remain single for the rest of my life, necessarily. I'm just not in any hurry to find a husband."

"Because you're still in mourning?"

"Not in the way you might think." She sighed, not sure she wanted to explain; not sure if he was capable of understanding, even if she tried.

How could mere words convey the tragedy of a once-vital man fading away, or the triumph of human dignity in the face of suffering? How to explain that Derek's courage had been an inspiration which had kept her afloat in the months following his death?

But Liam wasn't inclined to drop the subject. "Now you've got me curious. Care to elaborate?"

"I loved my husband dearly, but his death came as a relief. Watching him deteriorate drained me, too. I knew how he hated his reliance on others. It hurt to see former friends drift away, to watch him become more isolated in the prison of his disease. How could I claim to love him and at the same time want him to remain alive for my purely selfish reasons?"

"That was never your choice to make," Liam said with surprising insight. "You were just as much a prisoner as he was, and just as much a victim of his illness.''

His ability to go straight to the heart of things in a way that friends had not been able to do left her throat suddenly thick with tears.

''Yes,'' she said, hanging on to her composure with a supreme effort. ''We prepared for his death together and after, when the formalities were done with, I set out as we'd agreed I should, to make a new life. But words are easy. It's the doing that's hard. As the sadness at his dying diminished, I became so…angry at the way we'd been cheated. We'd once shared so many dreams for the future, and I found I couldn't let go of them. I clung to them because doing so kept the memory of him, as he used to be, alive in my heart. I didn't want to remember him as he'd been at the end.''

''It's natural enough to want to hang on to the good times, Jane. They're what keep us going when misery threatens to take over.''

''I know. But it meant that, after adjusting to the loss of a very sick husband, I spent another year mourning the loss of that other man, the one who'd been so *alive,* who'd waited at the altar for me, who'd whisked me off to Bali for our honeymoon, who'd taken me white-water rafting down the Fraser River, who'd played tennis with me at the club and ridden elephants with me in Thailand.''

She hadn't even realized she was crying until the tears splashed down the front of her shirt. She searched through her pocket for a tissue and when she didn't find one, scrubbed at her face with her fingertips while Liam sat and watched.

''You could at least offer me something to wipe my

nose with," she sniffled, embarrassed by his unwavering gaze.

"There's a box of tissues inside on the coffee table. Help yourself."

Grateful for the excuse to escape, she scuttled away to mop up the damage. When she came back out again, she brought the plates and other paraphernalia for the meal with her. Liam was lifting scarlet-shelled rock crabs out of the pot and arranging them on a metal tray, but he stopped to watch as she laid everything out on the picnic table.

"Didn't anyone ever teach you that it's rude to stare?" she inquired irritably, trying not to squirm in the face of his continued scrutiny.

He dismissed the question with a nonchalant shrug. "It's okay to cry, you know. Everyone does, at one time or another."

"Not you," she said, busying herself setting the table. "I bet you can't remember the last time you broke down in tears."

"Yeah, well, for once, we aren't talking about me. We don't have to talk about you, either, if it's so painful."

Her hands stilled. In fact, every part of her seemed to grow quiet—less because of what he said than at how he said it. Once again, he'd caught her off guard with his rare kindness. "Actually, it's not. I don't really know what started me crying just now."

It was a lie, but she didn't dare tell him the truth: that his implicit understanding of everything she'd said had triggered the outburst.

"What most people don't understand," she said, "is that once a person gets past the mourning stage, she needs time to replenish herself before moving on to the next phase in her life. It's only been in the last six months or so that I've come out the other end of the tunnel, as it were, but my friends immediately made it their mission to pair me up with another potential husband. They can't accept that I'm happy just to be alone for a while.''

"Makes perfect sense to me." He gestured at the tray. "Dinner's ready. We can eat out inside, if you're finding it too chilly.''

"Out here is fine."

He threw another log on the fire, then rolled his chair next to where she sat at the table. "So, what else are you, besides a widow?" he asked, refilling their glasses. "What do you do, when you're not on vacation?''

"I'm the loans manager at a suburban bank branch in Vancouver. I went back to work right after the funeral. At the time, it seemed the best thing—keeping busy, and all that—but since the beginning of the year, I've had one cold after another and in May came down with a really bad bout of the flu which turned into pneumonia. My doctor recommended a complete change of pace for a while, so I've taken a three month leave of absence. I plan to do nothing but soak up the sun and laze away the days until September." She angled a glance at him. "What about you? Why are you here?''

"Because I'm not much use at work right now. I'd have thought that was obvious.''

"Only to someone who knows exactly what kind of work you do. From the little you've told me, I'd guess you're some sort of structural engineer.''

"Bingo! Go to the top of the class, Janie.''

"But there's surely more to the job than fixing damaged oil rigs?"

"You're right. It's not all fieldwork. I spend my share of time in my Vancouver office, working on designs. But let's get back to you. I wouldn't have pegged you as someone wanting to compete in what's traditionally been a man's world."

"But that's half the fun," she said, dipping a chunk of succulent crabmeat in melted butter. "I like to think that, as a woman, I bring an added dimension of sensitivity to the job. Asking to borrow money is never easy."

"You don't think men can be sensitive, too?"

"Of course I do. And if I hadn't known it before, you certainly taught me differently tonight."

"Oh, don't go all soft on me, or that'll be your last glass of wine! Just because I lent a sympathetic ear for a change doesn't change the basic rules we've laid down about not getting involved in each other's lives."

Planting her elbows on the table, she cradled her glass and regarded him solemnly. "Why is it so difficult for you to admit that you're not all hard edges and tough attitude? Is it because you're afraid, if you let your guard down, that I'll take advantage of you?"

He let out a bellow of laughter. "That'll be the day! I might be in a wheelchair, but I can still run the other way if I have to."

She leaned toward him and beckoned him closer. "Don't worry, Liam," she whispered. "Your precious bachelorhood is safe with me. I won't try to spin a casual, spur of the moment invitation to dinner into something more than it's meant to be. And just to prove it, I'm not even going to offer to wash the dishes before I leave."

"You might want to wash your face though," he said. "You've smeared melted butter all over your chin."

She sat back with a scowl. "There's no getting in the last word with you, is there? You always have to come back with some smart put-down."

"Would you rather I hadn't told you? Most of the women I know are vain enough about their appearance that they want to know things like that."

"But I'm not one of those women. You don't know me at all."

For a moment, he looked at her, his gaze skimming from her ankles to her face and settling with disconcerting thoughtfulness on her mouth. As if, maybe, he was debating kissing her. As if, for all his abrasive denials, he found her attractive.

Then, expression unreadable, he said, "You're right. I don't know you, nor do I intend to. Circumstance has made us neighbors but that doesn't make us friends. Eventually, we'll leave here and go our separate ways. As far as I'm concerned, the sooner that happens, the better."

She left shortly after that, and why not? His last remark had hardly invited further conversation.

He'd been glad to see her go. Asking her over had been a mistake, one he'd make sure he didn't repeat. He'd watched the pale shape of her fade into the night with the utmost relief.

Pity he couldn't as easily dismiss her from his mind. Long after the light had gone out in her bedroom and the fire pit had grown cool, he remained outside, alone with the memory of her.

I'm not one of those women, she'd said.

No, he thought, tilting his head to look at the stars, she was different from the rest. Too honest. Too vulnerable.

When she'd cried, he'd found himself chafing at his inability to get up and go to her. Times like that, a woman needed to be held. She'd been too long without that. Too long without a man's arms around her; without his hard, strong body to lean against.

Just as well he hadn't been able to take on the job. She didn't need another cripple, and the last thing he needed was the distraction of a woman like her. He might enjoy her fire, the spirit with which she challenged his opinions and attitude, but her gentleness terrified him.

Restless, frustrated, he wheeled across the grass to the path leading down to the dock. Jeez, what he wouldn't give to be able to shove the blasted wheelchair into the water and just take off on two good legs! To be able to walk again—to do as he pleased, whenever it pleased him!

The powerboat rocked gently at its mooring, but it was to the dinghy that he turned, heaving himself on one leg to the edge of the wharf and lowering himself to the thwart. He needed physical exercise, something demanding and strenuous enough to make him forget that he'd been reduced to half a man.

Releasing the mooring line, he picked up the oars and pushed off. Beyond the shadow of the dock, the bay lay silent and empty, the water as smooth as glass. Bending to his task, he propelled the dinghy swiftly forward, charting a course parallel to land.

It was just as he rounded the outcropping of rock which separated her stretch of beach from his when she suddenly surfaced not more than ten feet away, rising out of the sea slender and completely naked.

She was facing the other way, toward the shore, and did not see him. Resting on the oars, he watched as she raised one arm and lifted the wet hair from the back of her neck.

She was too thin. Even by starlight, he could see that. Her waist was a child's, her hips a mere suggestion of a woman's curves. Yet she was lovely. Fragile as porcelain. Desirable.

The sudden ache in his groin infuriated him. Not because of his body's response—handicap notwithstanding, he was, after all, still a man with a man's normal urges—but because it put the lie to what he'd been telling himself all evening.

He wanted her. God help him, *he wanted her!*

As if he'd shouted out the message at the top of his lungs, she turned and caught him watching her.

CHAPTER FOUR

HER eyes widened in shock. Her hands flew up to cover her breasts even as she dipped low in the water to conceal herself from him, until the only part showing was her head, sleek and dark as a seal's, and the pale oval of her face.

Her whisper condemned him louder than if she'd screamed her outrage to the night. "Pervert! If this is the way you get your kicks, it's small wonder your wife left you for someone else! You're nothing but an overgrown teenager masquerading as a man."

"Hey," he said, "it was an accident. I didn't come looking for you, I came out to work off a few calories. I thought you were in bed. Your place has been in darkness for hours."

"How do you know that?" She bobbed a little closer to the boat, the ripples she sent shimmering over the surface of the water doing an excellent job of camouflaging her nakedness. "Do you sit there spying on my every movement?"

"Oh, give me a break, Jane! Yours is the only place for miles around. I don't have to be some sort of sick voyeur to notice whether or not the lights are on next door. And since we *are* such close neighbors, you might think twice before you decide to going skinny dipping again if you're going to get this bent out of shape at being caught in the raw."

"You are without doubt the most offensive creature I've ever met!" she gasped, teeth chattering with cold.

54

"I can't believe I was stupid enough to think you might be worth getting to know."

"And I can't believe we're having this conversation, here, at this hour of the night. For pity's sake, swim ashore before you succumb to hypothermia. I don't relish finding your body washed up on the beach in the morning. Contrary to what you might believe, I place a rather high value on human life."

"Especially mine, I'm sure!" she retorted, backing away from the dinghy. "Why else would you be stalking me like this?"

"Heck, Janie, I don't have to settle for modest little maidens like you when I've got an itch that needs scratching! There are plenty of other women only too happy to accommodate me."

"If they're that thick on the ground, why didn't you ask one of them to dinner, instead of me?"

"I already told you. No other reason than because you were there. If a roll in the hay was what I'd been looking for, I'd have gone elsewhere." Even though he couldn't see much of anything, he leaned forward and made a slow inspection of her indistinct shape. "Frankly, you're a bit too much on the skinny side for my taste and could use some fattening up. I've known greyhounds with more meat on their bones."

"And you're a disgusting pig," she said, slapping a handful of water in his face.

By the time he'd stopped chortling, she was ashore and running up the beach to the shadow of the trees lining the path to her house.

His laughter followed her all the way home, taunting, derisive. How pathetic he must find her, and small wonder! She didn't need him to tell her she didn't have what it took to appeal to a man. The mirror didn't lie, and the few pounds she'd gained over the last weeks did little to disguise her scrawny frame. As he'd so bluntly pointed out, not Liam McGuire's kind of woman at all.

The question was, why did she care? She'd never been the casual affair type. Derek had been her only lover and she'd been a virgin when they married. A man who discarded women as easily as he attracted them wasn't for her. If she ever fell in love again, it would be with someone who took monogamy as seriously as she did. *An itch that needed scratching* indeed! What kind of disrespect for women did a remark like that show?

And yet, when morning came, she found herself looking across the curve of the bay to the other house. Found herself thinking about the man who lived there. Hoping their paths would cross again—and dreading that they would.

He clearly wasn't anxious to run into her. Occasionally, she saw him from a distance, hauling his crab trap onto the wharf, or wheeling himself along the low bluff below the cottage. But he never once looked her way and there was no telling if they'd ever have exchanged another word if it hadn't been for the day of the storm.

She'd awoken that morning to a day of bruised skies and the kind of oppressive heat that promised trouble. Even with the doors and windows open wide, the house was like an oven. Thunder muttered in the distance, a forerunner of bigger things to come.

Just after three that afternoon, she heard the purr of an engine and saw Liam at the wheel of the powerboat, speeding away from the dock and out into the unprotected waters of the Sound.

"He must be crazy," she exclaimed, stunned. "Doesn't he know the danger of being out at sea with ugly weather like this closing in?"

Within an hour of his leaving, the thunder rolled down Bell Mountain, full of fury. Not long after, the heavens opened and the mist swept in, veiling the island so thoroughly that even the wild red poppies growing at the foot of the porch steps looked faded.

By five, the flowers were bent flat by the rain sheeting down, their heads pressed into the sodden earth. By six, a premature dusk threatened the afternoon light.

Throughout it all, between the deafening cracks of thunder and during the brilliant flashes of lightning, Jane strained to hear the throaty growl of an engine; to detect through the densely swirling mist the outline of a boat's hull next to the dock. There was nothing. Nothing but nature on a wild summer rampage.

Bounder was the one who finally found him. Tired of his restless pacing, she'd let the dog out during a lull in the weather, expecting he'd soon decide he'd rather be inside where it was dry. But minutes passed with no sign of him, adding another anxiety to that already chewing holes in her peace of mind.

When at last he showed up, he refused to come into the cottage, choosing instead to circle agitatedly at the foot of the porch steps and give vent to short, high-pitched yelps so different from his usual deep bark that she knew at once something was amiss.

His message was clear enough. *Come with me!*

Grabbing her grandfather's oilskin jacket from the hook behind the door, she flung it over her shoulders and set out. Immediately, the dog made for the beach, running ahead of her and stopping every few yards to make sure she was following.

The tide was low, the rocks slippery, the mist so thick that she'd have lost her bearings had the dog not been there to guide her up the low bluff on the far side of the cove, to where the path forked, with one way pointing directly to the dock, and the other to Liam's place.

It was there, as she stopped to catch her breath, that the mist thinned just enough for her to discern the powerboat, safe at its mooring. Just a few feet away and angled steeply because of the low tide, the ramp spanned the space between land and water.

And midway between the two, on the worn, rain-slick boards, an empty wheelchair lay tipped on its side.

As though satisfied that it had wreaked havoc enough for one day, the storm seemed suddenly to abate. The thunder, the rain, the hectic beat of her heart—they all stopped, leaving behind a stillness made all the more terrifying because the only sound to penetrate the silence was the uneven spatter of water dripping from the trees.

No cry for help. No urgent splashing to disturb the oily calm of the sea lapping idly against the hull of the boat. No sign at all of anyone but herself and her dog. They might have been the only two living creatures left on earth.

She would have stood there indefinitely, paralyzed with fear, had Bounder not lost patience with the delay and harassed her into moving on—not, thank God, toward the water, but to the house whose roofline appeared briefly as the malicious mist shifted inland.

Liam lay sprawled on the porch, his shoulders

propped against the wall, and one hand massaging his injured leg.

Well, at least he was alive!

Relief had her babbling with rage. "You idiot!" she shrieked, dropping to her knees beside him. "What were you thinking of, taking off in weather like this?"

His lips barely moved when he answered. "I had an errand that needed taking care of."

"An *errand?*"

He gave a weary sigh. "I needed to get to a phone to leave a message for someone, if you must know, and my cell unit's conked out on me."

Astounded, she exclaimed, "What on earth kind of phone call was worth risking your life for?"

"None of your business," he said.

She sat back on her heels and planted her fists on her hips. "Is that a fact? Well, let me tell you what *is* my business. *You* acting irresponsibly and leaving *me* to handle the consequences. Did you once stop to consider what I've gone through all afternoon, wondering whether I should send up flares to alert the coast guard to start a search and rescue operation, or whether I should leave you to wallow in your own stupidity? You have no right—no right at all...!"

She stopped and drew breath, furious to find herself trembling and on the brink of tears. *I can't do this,* she thought. *I can't afford to get involved with this man and his problems. I can't worry about whether he lives or dies. I don't have what it takes to cope with another soul in crisis.*

"Ah, Janie," Liam said, lifting his head a fraction and regarding her from beneath drooping eyelids, "you were worried about me. How nice!"

"Don't make a joke out of this," she quavered. "It's

anything but funny. What if you'd run aground in the fog and the boat had started taking in water? What then, with you in your condition?"

"Calm yourself," he said wryly. "It didn't happen. Unfortunately for you, I survived unscathed."

"You call the state you're in 'unscathed'?" she flung at him. "I happened to see the wheelchair. I know how far you had to crawl to get back here. You're scraped and bleeding, and probably black and blue all over, and it's no less than you deserve. If I had a grain of sense, I'd leave you here to rot."

"Why don't you, then?"

"Because, unlike you, I'm not totally wrapped up in myself and my own problems. My conscience won't allow me to simply walk away and leave you in the state you're in."

"Oh, goody!" he sneered. "Just what I need— Florence Nightingale with a halo, riding to my rescue!"

"Count yourself lucky that I've taken enough first-aid courses to know what to do."

He was hurting and he was exhausted, and nothing he could affect in the way of sarcastic bravado could hide the fact. But that didn't stop him from leering at her and saying, "Are you going to give me mouth-to-mouth resuscitation, Janie?"

"No," she said, eyeing his injuries. On closer inspection, she saw that he'd smacked the side of his face, probably when the wheelchair had tipped over. But of more immediate concern were the gravel and slivers of cedar embedded in the wounds he'd inflicted on himself as he'd crawled back to the cottage. *They* were an infection in the making. "By the time I'm finished with you, you're probably going to need it, though. Even if you haven't suffered any other injuries, those scrapes need attention.''

"I can hardly wait," he said morosely.

She pushed herself to her feet. "Good. We'll begin by getting you out of those clothes and dried off. You're soaked to the skin."

"Forget it," he said, shying away from her as if she had typhoid. "You're not taking advantage of me when I'm in no position to defend myself. Keep your hands to yourself."

"Don't flatter yourself," she shot back. "It's not you personally I care about. I'd be just as concerned about anyone—though most people would have shown more sense than to act the way you have."

"That's me," he said sourly. "Always looking for trouble and usually managing to find it, one way or another. Go away and leave me alone, for Pete's sake. Drowning would have been preferable to listening to you carrying on like a harpy."

She opened her mouth to agree, but the flippant reply died on her lips. For all his tough talk, there was no mistaking the whiteness around his mouth, the dullness in his eyes, that came of bearing up under pain.

"I'm not going anywhere, Liam McGuire, no matter how many insults you throw at me," she told him. "You need help and there's no one else around to dish it out but me. Like it or not, I'm getting you inside and I'm looking after you, so instead of wasting your energy arguing, use it to get to your feet. Can you stand, do you think, if you lean on me?"

"Yes, I can stand," he snarled. "I'm not a complete cripple, damn it! I can move about under my own steam."

"Then prove it."

The glare he directed at her was enough to sour milk, but she refused to be intimidated. "Save the black looks for someone who cares," she said, staggering a little as he heaved himself upright and slung an arm over her shoulder. "This isn't the Academy Awards and even if it were, I'm fresh out of Oscars."

"You're a mean-mouthed witch, you know that?"

"Yes," she said, dismayed by his pallor and the sweat beading his brow. "You have a way of bringing out the worst in me."

He was well over six feet and muscular, a big, strong man unused to having to depend on a woman. He hated the indignity of being handicapped and despised every laborious second it took for him to hobble across the porch and into the house.

Once there, he used the furniture to take some of his weight but by then the toll had begun to tell. What it cost him to preserve his infernal male pride showed only in the grim line of his jaw and his labored breathing. He would have swallowed broken glass before he'd have admitted to the agony he was suffering.

"Where do you think you're going?" he panted when she went to steer him past the table to the door on the far wall.

"Where do you suppose? I'm putting you to bed."

"Like hell!" he said rudely, staggering to the sofa and collapsing in an exhausted heap. "Just leave me here and let me get on with things by myself."

"And how do you propose to do that? You're in so much pain you can hardly sit up. So put a lid on the macho act and tell me where you keep your medication."

"No pills," he said, turning his face away.

"What do you mean? You *do* have something for pain control, I hope?"

"Enough to start my own pharmacy," he said grimly, "but I'll be damned if I'm letting you dope me up for something as minor as this."

"I should have figured you'd say that. Well, what about towels—or don't you believe in using them, either, unless you're up to your neck in water?"

"Woman," he ground out, closing his eyes as if that might make her evaporate into thin air, "you're trying my patience to the limit. Please, for the last time, get the blazes out of my house and leave me alone. I don't want you here. I don't need you. I don't need anything but a bit of peace and quiet."

"The towels, Liam," she said implacably.

He dropped his head to his chest and sighed, a great, heaving exasperated exhalation of defeat that blew like a breeze through the stuffy room. "Over there." He gestured to a tall cabinet in the corner.

"Okay," she said, taking out two large bath sheets. "These look up to doing the job. Come on, let's get those wet jeans and shirt off."

His head jerked up as if he'd been poked with a cattle prod. "You've got to be joking!"

"No," she said, removing his soggy boating shoes. His long, tanned feet were icy to the touch and the skin on the side of his ankles had been scraped raw from his arduous trek up the ramp to the house. "I'm perfectly serious. Whether you want to admit it or not, you're in shock and you need to be kept warm."

"Not by you, Janie," he said balefully. "You're not stripping me down to my skivvies and checking out my equipment."

She smothered a laugh. "Then undress yourself."

"I will," he said, but made no move to do so.

"Well?" She looked at him expectantly. "What are you waiting for?"

"You," he said. "Turn around."

"Oh, for heaven's sake—!"

"*Turn around!* Better yet, go wait on the porch."

"How about I boil some water for coffee and get the first-aid kit out, instead?"

He rolled his eyes in despair. "Whatever! Anything to stop your nagging. Just don't try sneaking a peek."

"I wouldn't dream of it," she said. "I can't imagine you've got anything I'd be interested in seeing, anyway."

"You wish!"

She turned away to hide a smile. Didn't he realize that, if she'd been all that desperate to see what he was so eager to hide, all she had to do was look in the shaving mirror hanging over the sink? But where was the point when, even if she'd had hopes of something more than simply tending his scrapes, he was in no shape to fulfill them?

"You appear to be having difficulties," she remarked at the cursing and various rustlings going on behind her. "Are you sure I can't help?"

"You can help," he muttered savagely. "You can call off your damned dog. I don't need my ears washed."

"Don't be so ungrateful. I'd never have found you if it hadn't been for him."

"Remind me to show my appreciation the next time I'm looking for crab bait." More rustling, less harsh this time, and something hit the floor with a soft thud; his wet jeans probably. "There! I'm done. You can bring on the Band-Aids."

He was naked from the waist up but had managed to wrap one towel snugly around the lower half of his body, including his legs and feet. All she could think was that if what he'd covered was a tenth as impressive as what he chose to display, it was just as well he'd been seized by pride-induced modesty. Because she'd have stared, no doubt about it! He was....

She swallowed and veered her gaze away from the sculptured planes of the torso in front of her. *He was magnificent!*

Of course, she reasoned, diverting herself by laying out gauze pads and antiseptic, part of her reaction lay in the fact that she'd never seen him without clothes before. He always wore jeans and a shirt of some sort. And it was difficult to gauge a man's build when he was in a wheelchair. But the hardness of him...the power and strength!

Regarding her covertly and, she feared, reading her thoughts only too accurately, Liam inquired, "Something wrong, Janie?"

"Not a thing," she said hoarsely. "Let's get started."

Gently, she swabbed at his face. "You're going to have a black eye by morning."

"It won't be the first time," he said, flinching at the sting of the antiseptic.

That, though, was the easy part. The palms of his hands and the underside of his forearms were speckled with fragments of creosote-impregnated cedar. "These slivers have to come out," she said, wielding a pair of tweezers and turning her thoughts firmly away from the smooth, tanned flesh and solid musculature of his arm, "otherwise they'll become infected for sure."

"Hey, you're not drilling for gold, you know!" he

yelped at one point as she dug out a particularly stubborn splinter lodged in his palm.

"Keep still and stop being such a baby," she scolded, applying hydrogen peroxide to the various puncture wounds. "I'm done at this end. Pull the towel up a bit and let me have a look at your ankles."

"No," he said flatly. "The towel stays where it is."

She glanced up at him in surprise. "For heaven's sake, Liam, I'm talking a couple of inches only. Even *you* can't be that well-endowed!"

But he was in no mood for humor. "Leave it," he said, his expression so closed that she knew there was no point in persisting. "You've done enough, and I've *had* enough for one day."

Mystified, she shrugged and closed the first-aid box. "If you say so. But if you want my advice—"

"I don't." He shrugged irritably and combed his fingers through his still-wet hair. "It's not that I don't appreciate what you've done, but it's been a long day and I'm wiped out."

"Yes," she said. "I can see that you are. I'll make you something hot to drink, then I'll get out of here. Is coffee okay, or would you prefer soup?"

"Coffee will be fine."

"Of course. It'll take only a minute or two to make."

But that was more time than he had to spare. When she came back to the couch, he was snoring. His hands lay loosely at his waist, their red welts bright against the pale blue towel. His chest rose in deep rhythm with every breath he took. But it was his face which captured her attention. The unguarded expression; the spray of thick, dark lashes shadowing his eyelids; the curve of his mouth, more lenient in repose than anything he betrayed when he was awake—they touched her in a way she hadn't known for a very long time.

Leaving the coffee on the table, she went into the bedroom and returned with his sleeping bag. Careful not to disturb him, she covered him for, with the passing of the storm, cooler air had come in from the sea and the room would be cold by morning.

His earlier pallor had gone, replaced by a flush of color. Cautiously, she bent and slid her fingers lightly over the welt near his eye and down to his jaw. He was not feverish. His breath fanned her cheek, intimate as a caress.

Was that what prompted her to lean closer and kiss him? Or was it a sudden hunger to discover the inner man she'd never met before, the one who revealed himself to her only in sleep?

She'd intended a peck on the cheek, but somehow she found his mouth instead and lingered there. His lips were firm and cool and utterly unresponsive beneath hers. He was so deeply asleep, he'd never know the shameless liberty she'd taken, and just as well because the impulse had left her awash with a mess of emotions she didn't dare begin to explore.

Shaken, she turned off all but one small lamp and tiptoed out to where Bounder lay waiting for her on the porch, Liam's soggy shirt dangling from his mouth.

She could dish out punishment better than any woman he'd ever known. Touching him with her soft, pretty hands. Stroking her fingers up his arm and over his face. Making him want things he couldn't have—like turning his back on lessons too well learned to be shoved aside on the strength of nothing.

Because that was what he amounted to these days. Nothing! And he'd been coping well enough with that, until she showed up on the scene.

I'm fresh out of Oscars, she'd said in that superior, know-it-all way of hers, but he'd fooled her with his performance, nonetheless.

Just as well she was such an innocent. A more experienced woman would have realized in a flash that the only part of him apparently unmoved by her impromptu kiss lay above the waist—and even that had taken uncommon willpower on his part!

She was dangerous—all the more so because she had no idea of the emotional punch she packed. It was time for him to move out of the line of her guileless fire, in which case perhaps this afternoon's aborted trip to Regis Island was a blessing in disguise, after all.

When he'd checked the message on his voice mail, just after lunch that day, the last thing he'd expected to hear had been a woman's breathy tones announcing, "Liam, it's Brianna. Tom finally caved in, not without persuasion I might add, and told me where you've disappeared to. The Thorntons have invited me to spend a couple of weeks with them on their motor cruiser just north of your island, so I thought I'd stop by for a quick visit on my way home—say two weeks from Saturday? I'm leaving tomorrow, so call me soon, darling, and let me know if this suits. Can't wait to see you. Kisses."

Furious with his friend and business partner for revealing his whereabouts, he'd hurled the phone across the room. But while they might be miracles of modern technology, cell phones weren't built to withstand the kind of abuse his had suffered. The impact when it landed had smashed the casing and put it out of commission for good, prompting him to take a run over to Clara's Cove to use the pay phone in the general store, despite the thunder rumbling in the distance.

At the time, risking getting caught in bad weather had struck him as the lesser of two evils.

Brianna Slater was a man-eating piranha and his first thought had been to put an end to any idea she had of landing on his doorstep, especially with him captive in a wheelchair. Only when he'd come close to capsizing the boat before he was halfway to his destination had he changed his mind and decided suffering her company was preferable to drowning. And on reflection, perhaps it wasn't such a bad idea because she'd surely dampen Jane's enthusiasm for his company. Brianna wasn't one to tolerate competition.

Wincing, he eased to a sitting position and flexed his bad leg. It hurt. The damned thing always hurt. But no worse than usual, and for that he would be forever grateful to whatever god had been looking out for him. When the chair had started its crazy backward slide on the greasy ramp, he'd known a terror worse than anything he'd felt at the time of the accident that had almost maimed him for life.

Understand this, they'd told him when they'd released him from the hospital. *You're lucky you've still got two legs. Don't push your luck. You've had your share of miracles. Rehab's going to be long and arduous. Don't try rushing it if you seriously expect to walk again without a cane.*

A fat lot they knew!

He swung his good leg to the floor then tenderly lowered the other and attempted to stand, easing himself up as carefully as if he were balancing on eggs.

Still, tongues of fire seared the length of his bad leg, severe enough that even he couldn't contain a groan.

Clamping his teeth together, he waited for the agony if not to pass, then at least to subside to a dull roar. It did not. It gouged holes in his pain threshold until the sweat poured down his face and he was shaking from head to foot.

Son of a bitch!

Defeated, he fell back down on the cushions, out of breath and out of patience. A chill crept over his skin as the sweating stopped. Exhausted to the point that even he was willing to admit it, he pulled the sleeping bag over himself and closed his eyes.

"Tomorrow," he promised the shadow-filled room. "Tomorrow I'll start over again. I'll get this thing licked or die trying."

CHAPTER FIVE

OVERNIGHT, the throbbing in his leg settled into the dull ache of what, for him, had become normality. Awaking to a morning that was clear and pleasantly cool, he inched to a sitting position and gingerly flexed his toes.

So far, so good!

The crutches were under the bed. He'd packed them, along with all the other paraphernalia that went with being crippled, despite his doctors's grave warnings that he wasn't going to need them for at least another three months. "I'll be the judge of that," he'd informed them.

Hopping on his good leg and dragging the other along as best he could, he made it to the bedroom, dressed, hauled out the crutches for the second time—the first had been when little Miss Goody Two-shoes got herself stuck up a ladder—and hobbled back to the kitchen, victorious. Hell, they were a piece of cake! If he'd known it was going to be this easy, he'd have used them sooner.

Whistling, he set the kettle to boil for coffee and opened the front door, figuring he'd take a couple of practice runs up and down the porch before venturing farther afield. With any luck, he'd be mobile enough to hike along the path heading north, away from her house, before she was up and about. The last thing he needed was her flapping around him and dishing out unasked-for advice.

Luck deserted him the minute he clumped outside. There on the porch was his wheelchair. In it was a basket of muffins still warm from the oven, with a note attached.

Hope you had a good night. Will stop by later to make sure you're okay.

"I don't think so, honey," he muttered, glaring at the muffins. If they'd been bran, he'd have tossed them over the railing without a second thought. But she'd filled them with raspberries and some sort of spice that had his mouth watering. *The way to a man's heart* and all that!

Only one thing to do: forget the coffee, along with any other ideas of a leisurely start to the day. He needed to be out of there fast, before she showed up, and hope she got the message.

Not that that was too likely, he reflected gloomily. She was too overflowing with the milk of human kindness, not to mention feminine wiles.

Unable to resist, he grabbed one muffin before heading inside again. His backpack hung on a coat hook behind the door. Quickly, he stuffed in a nylon windbreaker, a bottle of water, a can of nuts, a couple of chocolate bars. Passing by the wheelchair on his way out again, he eyed the muffins, fought a brief and losing battle with his pride, and added a couple to his other supplies.

"Just for good measure," he explained to the world at large, "in case I need an energy boost to get myself back in one piece."

Shortly after, he was on his way, swinging along the other end of the wraparound porch to the far side, and the steps which he hadn't been able to use before. Eight of them, a bit steeper-looking than they'd seemed when he'd viewed them from the wheelchair—but oh, brother, the freedom they offered!

The path below, running at a gentle incline away from the house, was broad; wide enough to take a car, almost. A couple of hundred yards farther along, it veered right, away from the sea, and disappeared into a belt of cottonwoods.

"Goal number one," he muttered, bracing himself for the descent. "Once out of sight under those trees, and I'm home free. She'll never find me."

When ten o'clock rolled around and there was still no sign of life at Liam's place, Jane gave up pretending she didn't care. This wasn't like him. She'd lived next door to him long enough to know he was an early riser. Welcome visitor or not, she'd have to investigate.

Once she'd reached the decision, urgency lent speed to her step. "Why did I wait so long?" she panted to Bounder, the nagging worry she'd tried to ignore bursting into full bloom as she slithered and slipped her hasty way over the wet grass. "What if he was more badly hurt than I realized? What if he's *dead?*"

If her heart hadn't been pounding so furiously, she'd probably have heard Liam sooner and realized that he was very much alive. As it was, when she first approached the cottage, all she noticed was the wheelchair, complete with basket of muffins, still on the porch, evidence enough, if proof was what she needed, that her fears were not without merit.

But the house was empty. The sleeping bag hung off the edge of the sofa and his wet jeans still sat in a heap on the floor. Either he'd managed to crawl into the bedroom, or he'd been kidnapped.

Then, it penetrated: from somewhere below the house, a string of curses that left the air so blue, it rivaled the sky. Racing back outside, she followed the din along the porch to the far side of the house.

When she arrived, Bounder was already on the scene and doing nothing to help matters. A crutch lay jammed in the open space between two steps. Another had slid down the bank and become tangled in the wild honeysuckle and stinging nettles. Midway between the pair and unable to reach either, Liam lay sprawled in the dirt at the foot of the stairs, feet facing the house, head resting on a backpack and pointing downhill.

Skidding to a halt, she pressed a hand to her heaving chest and surveyed the scene. No need to ask what had happened; it was clear enough. Like her, he'd discovered that the dew, combined with the remnants of yesterday's rain, made for unsafe footing. Unlike her, he'd fallen afoul of it.

Her first instinct was to rush to him. To cradle his head to her bosom and stroke back his dark, unruly hair, and murmur words of comfort and reassurance.

For once, she followed her second instinct.

"You really are out of your mind, aren't you?" she said conversationally, folding her arms and looking down on him from her lofty post at the head of the steps. "Have you always been inclined this way, or is it a fairly recent development?"

Red-faced, he glared at her. "Beat it, Janie! This is one party you're not horning in on."

"You'd like me to leave, is that it?"

He rolled his eyes heavenward. "Well, praise the Lord! She finally got the message!"

"No need to be sarcastic, Liam. I can take a hint, especially one delivered with all the subtlety of a charging bull."

Slowly, she descended the steps and retrieved the first crutch, then hooked one end through the top of the second and dragged it up the bank. Wedging both under her arm, she turned back the way she'd come. "Have a nice day," she said.

"Hey!" His bellow rang out across the quiet cove. "What the devil do you think you're doing with my crutches?"

"My goodness, Liam, I'd have thought even a man of your limited intelligence could figure that out! I'm taking them with me. It's the only way I can think of to put an end to your macho nonsense. But you can keep the backpack. From the looks of it, whatever was in there probably didn't survive the fall and won't be of much use in enabling you to take another stab at breaking your neck."

"Listen to me, you little witch—!"

"Keep it up," she said sweetly, "and I'll take the wheelchair, too."

"Over my dead body!"

"That can be arranged, Liam. In fact, at the rate you're going, you'll manage it all by yourself before the week's out."

His next explosion sent Bounder skittering for cover. "Don't you dare leave!"

She paused at the top of the steps and looked back over her shoulder. "Make up your mind, dear. Do you want me to stay, or not?"

"It would seem," he said, fairly gnashing his teeth with rage, "that what I want doesn't count for very much. Between you and this damned leg, I'm not left with a whole lot of choices.''

"They're the first sane words you've said today. Dare I hope there'll be more to come?''

"Oh, can the smart-ass remarks, Janie! I don't need them.''

"What do you need, Liam?''

Hooking his arm around the bottom step, he maneuvered himself semi-upright and stared out to sea. His expression was stony, proud.

"I'm waiting,'' she said, refusing to weaken.

Seconds—perhaps even a full minute—passed before he locked gazes with her and burst out, "For God's sake, woman! I'm already rolling around in the dirt at your feet. How much more do I have to grovel?''

Shame and pity swept over her then at the pain she saw in his eyes. It wasn't the physical suffering which was beating him down, but the affront to his dignity, to his self-reliance.

What had happened to her humanity, that she'd let herself get so caught up in the mean-spirited pleasure of showing him how helpless he was in the face of even the most minor adversity? Had her well of simple human kindness dried up completely with Derek's death?

"Forgive me,'' she said contritely. "I'm afraid I'm letting pride get in the way of common sense. Would you like…may I give you a hand up the steps?''

He gave a grunt of ironic laughter. "No, but if you've got a leg to spare, I could use that. Steps I can manage, as long as I stick to shuffling up and down on my backside. It's the stuff that sneaks up on me that makes me crazy. Like getting too cocky with those blasted things!'' He shook an impotent fist at the crutches, then began the laborious climb back up the steps. "I was doing...pretty well until I got... blindsided by the dew."

"Crutches take some getting used to," she said, aching to help him. "You might want to stick to flat ground for a while until you've really got the hang of them." Then, seeing the irate glower her advice produced, went on hurriedly, "But then, what do I know? If there's nothing else I can do for you, I'll be off."

"Not so fast, Janie!"

"Don't worry. I'll leave the crutches."

"I know," he said, a glimmer of humor replacing his scowl. "You'll leave the wheelchair, too. You might get a charge out of acting like a sergeant major, but you don't have the parts to really carry it off."

"I don't mean to boss you around," she said. "What you do is your business, after all. But knowing you're here, alone...." She sighed and lifted her shoulders apologetically. "Well, it worries me. You've come close to a serious accident twice in the last twenty-four hours, and this is such a remote spot. Steve's cottage, it's comfortable enough, but it's hardly the right sort of place...."

He'd reached the porch by then. Using the railing for support, he positioned the crutches and began swinging back the way he'd come. She had to hurry to keep pace with him. It was all she could do to keep her mouth shut and not tell him he should slow down, that this wasn't a race and he wasn't proving anything by covering the distance in record time.

"That's where you're wrong," he wheezed, pivoting himself around the corner to the southeast side of the house. "It's exactly right. Not the kind of luxury I'm used to, perhaps, but hey, if I wanted all the comforts of home, I could have stayed in town where all my well-intentioned, hale-and-hearty friends could come and slobber pity all over me.''

She noticed how glad he was to reach the hammock; how gratefully he lowered himself into it. ''Is there no one closer who could be with you? A family member perhaps?''

''No,'' he said, so decisively that she dared not question him further. ''If the refrigerator needs restocking, I can take the boat over to Clara's Cove. There's a swim ladder off the end of the dock so I can haul my sorry butt into the water and exercise my leg without stressing the joints. And the rest of the time....'' He favored her with a telling glance. ''I can vegetate, soak up the sun and enjoy the solitude.''

She pressed her lips together, her own pride rising to meet his. Finally, she said, ''Consider the message received. I won't bother you again.''

He was going soft in the head. After getting what he wanted—namely, rid of her—he found himself wishing she'd come back.

She didn't. But her dog did, every day for the next week. The benighted creature seemed to have developed a fondness for him which, to his horror, he found himself returning. Every morning, the mutt would show up and hang around, tongue lolling, tail wagging, brown eyes all moist with adoration. And he'd be glad of the company.

Cripes! He really must be losing his edge!

They developed a routine. He'd put himself through a daily system of rigorous strengthening exercises, during which time the dog would circle him, anxious as a mother hen with a backward chick.

When he sank, exhausted, into the hammock, Blunder would bring him whatever was closest at hand—a shoe, a stick, a tea towel drying on the railing—then settle down beside him and not move until noon, at which time he'd trot back to check things out at her place.

When Liam found himself considering kidnapping the creature, just to get her to come looking for it, he finally admitted defeat. He'd grown used to her sassy remarks, her smile, her concern—and yes, he might as well admit it—her cooking. Stale bread and cheese wore a bit thin, three days in a row, and he hadn't felt like fishing lately. Even taking the boat to Powell River on Vancouver Island, to get his phone replaced, had left him wasted. The rehab routine took too much out of him.

"Face it, buster," he told the lathered face staring back at him from the shaving mirror. "You miss her, plain and simple."

But he resisted doing anything about it for another week. If he was going to show up at her door, it wouldn't be on crutches. Spurred by that ambition, he doubled his exercise sessions.

Finally, on the Friday, with only a cane for support, he made the trek, taking the long way over the bluff because he didn't fancy losing his footing on the rocks lining the beach.

She was in the back garden, hanging laundry on one of those circular clothesline contraptions—bed linen and towels, transparent bits of underwear, a bikini so brief it practically qualified as a Band-Aid, and a nightshirt.

Approaching her house from the landward side, he saw her long before she noticed him. A couple of sheets flapping in the breeze camouflaged his arrival completely.

More beguiled than he cared to admit, he leaned against the trunk of the Douglas fir at the edge of the property and observed her. She was humming to herself as she worked, apparently perfectly content with the simple life she'd chosen. Every once in a while she'd reach up to reposition a clothespin or shake a piece of laundry into place.

Each time she did, he'd catch a glimpse of her breasts, smooth and sweet as ripe peaches, surging against the low-cut halter top she wore. And like some drooling old lecher on a street corner, he watched and waited in hope that the performance would be repeated.

Then the dog, which had stopped to follow some interesting scent or other, caught up with him and spoiled everything. Before he was exposed for the voyeur she'd once accused him of being, Liam moved from the shadows into the sunlight. "Excuse me, ma'am, do you do windows, too?"

She let out a little shriek and peered between the sheets, her eyes wide and startled. Then, recognizing him, she stepped away from the clothesline, one hand pressed to her throat. "Good grief, Liam, you scared me!"

All the suave openings he'd rehearsed evaporated at the unobscured sight of her. She'd definitely fleshed out since he'd last seen her. Her hips had rounded slightly, her collarbones protruded less sharply, the hollows under her cheeks seemed not as prominent.

She'd obviously been spending a lot of time outdoors. The sun had deepened her skin to honey-gold and left no sign of a tan line anywhere. Her dark hair had taken on a burnished sheen. Her legs....

"Yeah...well...." He cleared his throat and averted his gaze. Best not to dwell too long on her legs; they led to dangerous territory, "Sorry about that."

Dropping a handful of clothespins in the basket at her feet, she watched and waited as he moved toward her. "How are you doing?"

"How do you think?" He hefted his cane in one hand.

Joy, pure and simple, lit up her face. "Oh, my heavens! The crutches! You're standing on your own two feet...oh, Liam, how wonderful!"

If impressing her had been the force that had driven him to achieve impossible goals, it had been worth every miserable, aching minute just to bathe in the warmth of her undiluted pleasure. "Thanks," he said.

"Well!" She lifted her shoulders—a dangerous move, with those delicious breasts bobbing around like that—and spread her palms to the sky. "This calls for a celebration. I've got iced tea in the refrigerator. Would you care for some?"

"It'll do for starters," he said, following her along a vine-draped veranda, past a small, old-fashioned portable bath tub hanging from a nail on the wall, and into a kitchen facing the east side of the house.

As such rooms went, it was pretty basic, he supposed: a shallow sink, a propane-powered refrigerator and range, a dresser painted white and filled with blue pottery, and a pine table like the one in the house where he'd grown up. But she'd made it charming, with starched white curtains, a window box overflowing with orange and red nasturtiums, and a vase of wild roses on the table.

An open doorway in the middle of the wall opposite showed part of a living room, with a spiral staircase connecting to an upper floor.

"This is nice," he said, leaning on the cane and looking around. "I'd always assumed the layout over here was the same as my place, but you've got a lot more space."

She paused in the act of pouring the iced tea and said pointedly, "Which you weren't aware of until now, of course."

"No. I wasn't…ready to make social calls before."

"And now you are?"

"To a point. I felt like stretching my legs and thought I'd stop by to see how you're doing."

"Should I be flattered?"

He shrugged, the old familiar alarm bells clanging at the back of his mind. *Give a woman an inch of encouragement, and she took it to mean a lifetime commitment….* "Not particularly. It's been a while since we last spoke, that's all and I—"

"It's all right, Liam, you don't have to explain. We both know precisely how deeply you value your privacy."

"Seems we have that in common. You haven't been beating a path to my door, either, lately."

She laughed, and he found his gaze drawn to the shape of her mouth. He'd called her any number of unflattering names: uptight, bossy, interfering. But the word that came to mind at that moment was "sexy."

"I know when I'm not wanted," she said. "And if I hadn't quite figured it out, you certainly set me straight."

This wasn't how he'd envisaged their meeting, with him more or less standing there with his tongue hanging out, and her so…in charge. Bent on reestablishing the preferred order of things, he said, "As long as we both abide by the ground rules, where's the harm in spending a bit of time together?"

"Perhaps you'd better define exactly what you mean by 'spending a bit of time together,' just to avoid any misunderstandings."

"A glass of wine occasionally, morning coffee once in a while, stuff like that."

"Sounds exciting," she said, biting her lip to keep from laughing again.

"What were you expecting, Janie?" he said, miffed. "A marriage proposal?"

"No," she said. "I already told you, marriage is the last thing I'm looking for from a man like you."

Inexplicably ticked off by that reply, he snapped, "And why not? A less than perfect specimen not good enough for you?"

"Actually, it's some of your other qualities I find annoying."

"Such as?"

"For a start," she said self-righteously, "I don't like being called Janie."

"Humph! If that's the extent of your complaints—"

"And I don't care for your confrontational attitude."

"Me, confrontational?"

She smiled and made a big production of examining the ceiling.

"Me confrontational," he agreed.

Eyes dancing, she replied, "And me Jane."

He shook his head ruefully. "Talk about screwing up! I came over here to effect a truce and damn near started another war! I'd have done better to stay away."

"I'm glad you came," she said softly. "I've missed you."

She was more honest than he dared be; more generous, too. "Even though I'm such a bear most of the time?"

"You've had reason." Thoughtfully, she drew a line through the condensation beading her glass. "Now that you've made such headway, will you be leaving the island?"

"Pretty soon. My lease is up at the end of August. But I must admit, I'm in no great hurry to get back to the city."

"Me neither."

"So?" He leaned toward her. "Where do we go from here, Jane Ogilvie?"

"If I wasn't afraid you'd take the invitation the wrong way, I'd ask you to stay for lunch."

"I was kinda hoping that's what you'd do," he said. "I'm tired of cooking for myself."

"It's nothing much, just fruit and cheese, and homemade baking powder biscuits."

"Sounds like a feast to me."

"Have a seat on the front porch while I get it ready, why don't you?"

"Sure," he said, and wondered how come he'd never noticed before that she had dimples when she smiled.

She fairly fled back to the kitchen.

Stay calm! she told herself, knowing her cheeks were flaming with untoward pleasure. *You've been given the chance to start over with him. Don't mess it up by repeating past mistakes. Don't hover, don't fuss, don't smother him with attention. Be casually friendly and above all, maintain your distance.*

Easy advice, but so difficult to follow when every instinct screamed for her to turn a casual lunch into an occasion never to be forgotten. If only she'd known he was stopping by, if only she'd thought to stock her cupboards with something other than staples! Caviar with Melba toast and a good white wine would have added an elegant touch; a wedge of blue Castillo and a loaf of Italian bread, and apricots; espresso coffee and petits fours...!

But this was Bell Island, not Vancouver. There were no upscale markets, no specialty shops catering to gourmet tastes, only the general store at Clara's Cove and Don Eagle, the owner's son, who made a weekly run to the cottage and left her the basic supplies she needed. Ordinary things like shampoo and flour and sugar.

Doing the best she could with what was at hand— plums and a couple of ripe pears from the trees out back, cheddar cheese, watercress from the creek running along the edge of the property, and the biscuits she'd had the foresight to bake—she piled everything on the rickety wooden tea trolley her grandfather had made years before, and trundled the lot outside.

Liam lounged on the porch swing, idly fondling Bounder's ears, but did the gentlemanly thing when she appeared. "Here," he said, grabbing his cane and levering himself to his feet, "let me give you a hand."

"It's not necessary, really."

"Don't spoil my one moment of gallantry, Jane. It's been a long time since I was in a position to be the one offering to help someone else."

"Heaven forfend I should deny you, then! Take a plate and dig in." The careless little laugh she'd intended emerged as painfully self-conscious as a teenager's giggle. *Get a grip, Jane!* she ordered sternly.

"Considering you weren't expecting company, you've put on quite a spread," he said, sampling one of the biscuits. "I haven't tasted anything as good as this since I was a kid."

"Your ex-wife didn't like baking?"

"My ex-wife wouldn't know one end of a rolling pin from the other. The only time I ever saw her use an oven was to heat up something that she'd bought ready-made at the nearest deli. My grandmother, on the other hand, lived to cook. The way she saw it, if a boy wasn't permanently hungry, he was coming down with something. If she were alive now, she'd be stuffing me with food from morning to night in the fixed belief that fattening me up would perform miracles with my leg."

No mention of a mother or father, she noticed, but she daren't ask him about them for fear of spoiling the mood.

Instead, she said easily, "My grandmother's the one who taught me to enjoy cooking. I baked my first loaf of bread here when I was about seven. I suspect it turned out hard as a brick, but I remember my grandfather chewing his way through it and praising every mouthful."

And so the afternoon slipped past unnoticed, the way time does when two people start exchanging tidbits of personal history to expose the make-up of their separate identities. He'd grown up in Metchosin, on southern Vancouver Island, she learned, and spent his early boyhood roaming the nearby coast and countryside. He'd been something of a loner, had been hauled up before the school principal for skipping classes when he was ten.

"Couldn't see the point of spending the day in a stuffy classroom, when the sun was shining outside and there were trails to explore and fish to be caught," he said.

But he loved to read and play piano. "No TV at my grandmother's house. She didn't believe in it—was convinced it was a way for space aliens to spy on people. So I had to find other ways to keep myself entertained on long winter evenings, at least until I got to high school and team sports took up all my spare time."

She listened to him, enthralled by the play of expression on his face, the snippets of information that made up his past.

"Never did plan on getting married," he said at one point. "It just didn't fit in with the overall scheme of things. Should have listened to my instincts, instead of my hormones."

"Probably," she said, unnerved by the chill of disappointment his remark induced. What did she care about his views on marriage? It wasn't as if she had any interest in dragging him to the altar.

The conviction which would once have sustained the thought just wasn't there anymore, though. A kind of aching had taken its place; a pang of something horribly akin to desire, not simply for someone with whom to share her life but, appallingly, for this particular man, faults and all.

It's because he's here and I've got no one else for company, she rationalized. *If we'd met in the city, he wouldn't stand out in a crowd.*

But he would. She didn't need him to draw pictures

of his romantic past. His marriage might have failed, but he didn't lack for female companionship. What woman could remain immune to that direct blue-green stare of his, that rare, disarming smile?

"This is about as good as it gets," he remarked at one point, cradling his head in his hands and staring out at the brilliant afternoon. "Perfect weather, great view, good food, good company—for once, I'm content with what I've got."

I'm not! The thought swam into her mind with shocking clarity, and another right behind it. *I want more. I want to live again, to feel!*

Abruptly, he turned his head and pinned her in a gaze that missed nothing. "I'm doing all the talking. What about you, Jane? Is this place working the magic you'd hoped for?"

CHAPTER SIX

SHE smoothed her thumb over the fingers of her other hand. "I'd say so, yes. I'm ready to move forward with my life."

"What about children? I take it there aren't any?"

"No," she said. "We discussed the possibility but because of Derek's illness, we decided against it. Later, as his condition deteriorated, I was glad there was no one else needing my attention and I could make him the focus of my life."

"What about now? You ever regret that decision?"

Blindly, she tried to spin her thoughts back, to the memory of Derek; to recall every feature of his dear face, the love in his eyes, his last whispered words to her—anything to eclipse the outrageous thoughts suddenly filling her mind.

But Derek was part of the past, a fading ghost. He was—God help her, it hurt to admit it but there was no denying the truth!—he was not relevant to today and he played no part in tomorrow.

Liam, however...oh, Liam was vibrant and dynamic and *here!* He made her sparkle inside; made her want to grab hold of life with both hands, and reach out to a future she'd never envisioned.

Sighing, she scrambled to collect herself. She could never admit to him the thoughts she entertained, or tell him how desperately she longed for a baby. He'd misunderstand, just as he would if she told him how his coming to her the way he had that day had sent her heart soaring. "Children were never really an option. I knew that and I accepted it."

At least it wasn't an outright lie. But that hadn't stopped her yearning. And now, because of this vital, charismatic man, the longing rose up again. She saw them so clearly she could have drawn their pictures: a daughter with Liam's aquamarine eyes, a son tall and strong like his father...!

"What about you?" Desperate to divert the curiosity in his gaze, she turned the question back on him. "Do you and your ex-wife have children?"

"No," he said. "It wasn't an option for us, either, though for different reasons. My work took me away too much and she wasn't interested in raising a family. Reason enough to make sure you don't start one, as far as I'm concerned. Kids deserve to be wanted by both parents—and I should know."

Even if his words hadn't signaled that the conversation had touched a nerve, the sudden vehemence in his voice did. "I'm sorry," she said. "I didn't mean to rake up unpleasant—"

"You weren't to know." Scowling, he fixed his attention on some spot far out to sea. "It's not something I talk about as a rule but since the subject's come up, you might as well know. I was one of those one-night-stand products, a baby no one planned, with a guy whose name my mother didn't even know. She ditched me as soon as I was born and left my grandmother to raise me."

"Oh, Liam!"

"Stop feeling sorry for me," he said harshly. "I was luckier than a lot of other kids who don't have anyone else to pick up the unwanted pieces. My grandmother died when I was nineteen, but by then I'd finished the first year of my engineering degree and done well enough to qualify for scholarships to see me through the rest of university. My mother might not have thought I was worth a second thought, but my grandmother knew better. She went to her grave a proud and contented woman.''

"And your mother—did she ever...have you never...?"

"Never," he said flatly. "I'm not interested in knowing anything more about her than I already do, which is that she's a cheap, heartless bitch who thought nothing of dumping a two-day-old baby on someone else's doorstep." He grimaced. "Maybe that's the kind of woman I deserve. At least, that's the pattern I see emerging when I look back on my marriage."

Jane had no recollection of getting up from the Adirondack chair, no knowledge at all of how she came to be next to him on the porch swing, stroking his face and whispering urgently, "You're wrong, Liam. You deserve much better than that. You're a good man, a wonderful man. Your mother missed out on the best thing that ever happened to her when she gave you up. As for your wife, she must be mad to have left you for someone else."

His hand came up and covered hers. "Careful, Janie," he warned, his fingers so warm and supple that it was all she could do not to curl her own around them and bring them to her mouth and kiss them. "Next thing you know, you'll be telling me you like me."

I could love you!

Quickly, before the thought took shape in words, she pulled away from him. "Let's not get carried away just because we've managed to spend a couple of hours together without it turning into a free-for-all!"

"You're right." He picked up his cane and got up from the swing. "Better not push our luck, I guess. Thanks for lunch."

Wishing she'd kept her mouth shut, or if she had to speak that it could have been something to touch his heart the way he so easily touched hers, she stood up, also, and tucked her top into the waistband of her shorts. "I'll walk with you to the back path."

"Stay put and enjoy what's left of the afternoon. I made it over here under my own steam. I can make it back again."

"It's no bother. I have to bring in the laundry anyway."

"Suit yourself."

If I were to suit myself, I'd find a way to make you want to stay....

She turned her face away before he read the wanting in her eyes, and led the way through the house and out to the patch of lawn in the back. As she passed the clothesline, she caught at the fabric of her sundress. It felt soft as the rainwater in which she'd rinsed it, and smelled of the sweet, fresh air of summer.

Watching her, Liam said, "I've never seen you in a skirt."

"There isn't much occasion to wear one out here, but I enjoy dressing up a bit, once in a while." Self-conscious under his scrutiny, she swung the dress away from her and started unpinning the towels hanging next to it. "Silly of me, I suppose, considering I'm only dressing up for myself."

"Oh, I don't know. I'm beginning to get an itch for something a cut above the bucolic, too." Thoughtfully, he prodded at the dry grass with the tip of his cane.

"You ever been to that place on the other side of the island?"

"Bell Island Resort and Golf Club, you mean? Yes, occasionally."

"Is the dining room any good?"

"It's excellent."

"Want to go there for dinner tomorrow?"

An elegant evening out with Liam McGuire? Her pulse leaped at the prospect. "We can't," she said, flattening the surge of pleasure invoked by his suggestion before it ran amok. "The club's privately owned. You have either to be a member or an invited guest."

He gave her the kind of look one might turn on a singularly backward child. "I didn't ask if they'd let us in, Janie. I asked if you wanted to have dinner there with me."

More than anything! her foolish heart cried. "I…if you can arrange it then, yes, that would be very nice," she said primly.

"Then quit quibbling and meet me at the boat tomorrow at seven."

She'd received more courtly and certainly more enthusiastic invitations, but none that inspired quite such a reaction. What point in deriding herself for skewing the whole affair out of proportion, when her entire being hummed with anticipation. Liam McGuire had asked her out, and this time not because he'd caught more crab than he could eat but presumably because he'd enjoyed her company enough that afternoon that he was willing to repeat the experience. In public, yet!

And she didn't have a thing to wear!

Oh, the sundress fit her well enough, but it was plain to the point of dull. Like her life of late, it lacked ex-

citement and suddenly she was tired of it. A kind of
expectation sang in her blood, a kind of hope she
hadn't experienced in years. She wanted to look pretty
again; desirable, the way she had when she and Derek
first fell in love. It had been so long since she'd had
reason to look glamorous for a man.

At least she'd thought to pack a pair of heeled san-
dals, her legs were evenly tanned, and she'd stuffed a
manicure kit in with her measly supply of cosmetics.
If only she'd had the foresight to include a few pieces
of jewelry, or a wrap to throw around her shoulders to
protect her from the weather, should it turn cool.
Somehow, her grandfather's yellow oilskins didn't
quite fit the image she hoped to present.

She wasn't entirely without resources, though. There
was a storage closet tucked under one of the bedroom
eaves and at the back, an old trunk, stuffed with trea-
sures that went back to her great-grandmother's time:
long, flowing skirts and blouses with lace jabots; old-
fashioned button boots, and exotic Japanese sunshades;
costume jewelry studded with crystal and jet and
mother-of-pearl; lengths of chiffon and velvet which
had transformed Jane from princess to gypsy to fairy
queen on rainy summer afternoons when she was a
child.

They were all still there, smelling faintly of lavender
and patchouli and must.

She might as well have shown up in prison garb the
next night, for all the impact she made on Liam.

"You look different," he said, after he'd ordered a
bottle of Shiraz to go with their Chateaubriand.
"You're wearing stuff on your eyes."

Stuff? The hours she'd spent laboring over her appearance—airing out the gauzy, silk-fringed shawl, pinning her hair in a sleek coil and anchoring it in place with a silver comb, pinching her earlobes with lapis lazuli earrings as heavy as pigeon's eggs—all that amounted to nothing more than *stuff on her eyes?* "It's called mascara and eye shadow," she informed stonily.

"Uh-oh! I said something wrong?"

"Not at all."

"Why the fishy-eyed glare, then?"

"You're imagining things, Liam," she said, affecting nonchalance. "I'm perfectly delighted to be here and having a wonderful time. And just for the record, you look different, too. Positively clean, for a change."

In fact, in black slacks and a long-sleeved white shirt, he looked more handsome than the law allowed. Every woman in the place was eyeing him as if he were the star attraction on the menu, and she herself...oh, she was having difficulty not drooling!

He grinned. "Gee, thanks—I think!"

"I can only suppose your improved appearance is what persuaded them to let us in here tonight."

"They'd have let me in if I'd been in my birthday suit, Janie," he said smugly. "I have connections in high places. All that was required was a phone call to the right party, a small detail I took care of this morning. I never for a moment doubted we'd be allowed in." With a superbly negligent gesture, he indicated their table, wedged snugly between the dance floor and a window overlooking the sea. "Or that we'd be given one of the best spots in the house."

"How nice to be so sure of one's welcome," she said, the image of him wearing nothing but his smile nibbling great holes in her composure. "And how wonderful that you managed to get your cell phone working again. One wonders how one ever managed without such modern miracles.''

"One does, indeed!" Deriving great entertainment at her expense, he grinned sunnily. Then, when the attempt to charm her fell on stony ground, he reared back in his seat and said, "Does one have a lemon in one's mouth perchance? Or a bee up one's—?"

"Don't be vulgar, Liam."

"My apologies. Let me try to rephrase the question in such a way as not to offend your sensibilities." Smile fading, he tapped his altogether beautiful front teeth with his fingernail a moment, then said, "Something's got you badly bent out of shape. Is it the company you're keeping? Having second thoughts about being seen in public with me?"

"The idea has crossed my mind."

"How so? You seemed to think it was a good idea when I first mentioned it."

"It still could be," she burst out, furious with him because he was so obtuse, and with herself because she was ready to cry with frustration and disappointment. The evening was going down the tubes before it had properly begun! "Everything would be just fine if you weren't so…!"

"What? So clearly not your type?"

"No!" she exclaimed, throwing caution to the winds. "If you weren't so self-involved. I went to a lot of trouble to look special for you tonight, but do you even notice? Do you have the grace or wherewithal to offer a compliment? No! All you can come up with is that I've got 'stuff on my eyes'!"

"Would it make you feel more appreciated if I got

up and started thumping my chest with pride at having you as my date for the evening?''

"I'm not your date. Admit it, Liam, I'm just a convenient body living next door, and could just as well be bow-legged and cross-eyed for all you care."

"Not quite," he said. "I enjoy your company well enough, in small doses, and as long as you don't go overboard in your expectations of what our spending time together implies."

"Well, don't worry that I'm getting ahead of myself! I don't interpret tonight to be the prelude to a proposal of marriage, if that's what concerns you."

"That's good," he said. "Especially since all I had in mind was sharing a bottle of wine, a good meal, and a little adult conversation—the latter of which seems to be in rather short supply, I might add."

At that, she must have looked as devastated as she felt because all at once, he reached across the table and took both her hands in his. "You know, Janie, it's easy to imagine things that aren't really there when the options are limited. Chance has thrown us together, not choice. We're all each other has at the moment and as a result, we've become somewhat dependent on each other. But it would be a mistake for us to read more into it than that."

"Dependent? Speak for yourself," she said scornfully. "I don't need you for anything."

"Yes, you do," he said, with more kindness and insight than he'd ever shown before. "You're adrift in loneliness, whether you're ready to admit it or not. You're the kind of woman who needs other people in order to feel fulfilled. The kind who gives. And I— dammit, I'm in the position where I have to take more

than I care to, and we've developed a certain…relationship because of those things.''

Swallowing the ache in her throat, she said, ''Is that
such a bad thing, Liam?''

''It could be. Do you really think I don't know I'm
with the most beautiful woman in the room, or that I
don't find you desirable?'' He shook his head in mock
reproof. ''Heck, Janie, it would be very easy to make
a pass at you, to embark on an affair.''

''But it's not going to happen.'' She didn't need him
to complete the thought. He was clearly leading up to
letting her down gently.

Releasing her hands, he swirled the wine in his glass.
''If our lives were running along as usual, we'd have
nothing in common except, perhaps, a mutual distaste
for one another. Our paths would never have coincided.
We don't move in the same social circles. We don't
share the same goals or even similar interests. This
summer is an aberration, a time-out for both of us, and
it's important we recognize that it won't last forever.
In another week or two, maybe less, we'll go our separate ways and likely never see each other again.'' He
stopped and heaved a mighty sigh. ''So no, it's not
going to happen.''

''Well, thank you for spelling it out for me, but you
really didn't have to. I'd already arrived at the same
conclusion.''

''Then we're in agreement.''

''Absolutely.''

Indicating the Chateaubriand the waiter had carved
and set before them, Liam raised his wineglass. ''In
that case, let's drink to a fine meal and start eating
before this gets cold. *Bon appétit!*''

To say the rest of the meal was strained was to overstate the obvious. "Good little band they've got here," he remarked at one point, when the lapse in conversation became too oppressively obvious. "I hadn't expected they'd have live music."

"They don't, except during the summer and even then only on weekends."

"Ah, yes, you did mention you'd been here in the past. Were you with your husband?"

"A couple of times, when we were first married."

"If I'd known that, I'd have suggested we go someplace else. The last thing I wanted was to stir up unhappy memories."

The only unhappy memories, she could have told him, *are those we're creating tonight.* "It was a long time ago," she said starchily. "And there *isn't* anyplace else on the island."

He rolled his eyes in mock despair. "Struck out again, McGuire! Shall we talk about the weather, instead?"

"I'd just as soon not."

That dealt a death blow to any pretense they were having a good time! Giving up, he concentrated on his meal, his appetite clearly none the worse for the company he was keeping.

She could hardly say the same for her. The beef, delicious and tender though it probably was, might as well have been cardboard. That everyone else in the room was having a whale of a good time merely emphasized the pool of alienation in which the two of them were struggling to remain afloat.

Aware of his glance resting on her every once in a while, Jane fought to keep her expression calm and unruffled. But inside, she was bleeding. Not until he'd spelled out the way he viewed their relationship had she realized how big a part he'd come to play in her life. That he was right, and their connection would end with summer, was too painful to contemplate.

"You care for dessert?" he asked when their plates had been taken away.

"No, thank you."

"Coffee?"

She shook her head. "I'll pass."

He could barely contain his relief. "Then let's get out of here."

Indeed yes! Coming in the first place had been a mistake. They were the only two in the room who weren't a couple.

"Let's," she echoed miserably.

If the evening had ended then, with both of them sulking, she might have been saved from herself. For a minute, when he levered himself to his feet and reached for his cane, she thought she was safe from the silly dreams persisting at the back of her mind. She was in the grip of a late-onset adolescent infatuation, that was all; one based on nothing but proximity and, as he'd so bluntly pointed out, lack of choice.

But the music was fast, the rhythm infectious, and the tiny dance floor packed with people too busy enjoying themselves to notice the tiny drama taking place on the periphery of the crowd. As she went to pick up her wrap from the back of her chair, someone accidentally bumped Jane from behind, a glancing blow only, but catching her off guard and just a little off balance the way it did, it was enough to send her staggering.

With a gasp of shock, she collided into Liam. Automatically, he closed his hands over her shoulders to steady her, or perhaps even to hold her at a distance because heaven knew he'd made it plain enough he didn't want her crowding him.

Too late, though; that split second of contact, and the damage was done. The feel of him—the solid wall of his chest beneath her palms, his touch on her bare skin—sent shock waves of awareness ricocheting clean down to the soles of her feet.

The reaction seemed to be mutual. A tremor swept over him and she felt his breath, ragged at her temples. Daring to look up, she found him gazing down at her as if he'd just seen her for the first time.

For one startled moment, they remained that way, his eyes burning into hers, his face a mask of ill-concealed confusion as he fought whatever private demons pursued him. Then, with agonizing slowness, his hands slid down her arms until he found her fingers. Lacing them in his, he said hoarsely, "It would be a shame to let the entire evening go to waste. Let's dance."

"We can't," she said, too strung out to care about diplomacy or tact. "It's all you can do to walk with a cane. What if you fall and hurt your leg?"

"I won't, not as long as I've got you to lean on." A fleeting smile touched his mouth. "Unless, of course, you're embarrassed to be seen doing the shuffle when everyone else is cutting a high-stepping rug with the cha-cha."

As if it mattered one iota, she said on a frail breath, "They're not playing the cha-cha anymore."

"You're right," he said, holding her lightly at the waist. "They've switched to something even I can manage."

The question was, could she? Could she keep her soul intact, her heart where it belonged, with the clarinet player weaving a soulful blues number through the air and binding her ever more tightly to Liam? Could she control the runaway response of her body? Or should she stop trying to fight a war she couldn't hope to win and simply give in to the overwhelming urge to plaster herself all over him and let tomorrow and its repercussions go hang themselves? Did either of them have the fortitude to resist such blatant temptation?

The answer wasn't long in coming.

All evening, she'd avoided any kind of physical contact with him. Much though it had gone against her better nature, she'd stood back and let him struggle unaided, in and out of the boat and up the path to the clubhouse. He'd made it clear often enough that that was the way he preferred it. He managed by himself every other day, and just because he'd abandoned his customary blue jeans in favor of something a bit dressier didn't mean he couldn't cope the same as usual.

But now, having once touched each other, they couldn't seem to let go. As naturally as water runs downhill, his hands slid over her hips and locked in the small of her back. And just as naturally, her arms found their way around his neck to where his hair brushed the edge of his collar.

"You smell nice," he murmured, resting his chin on the crown of her head.

Nice. When they'd first sat down to dinner, she'd have rated the word only slightly above *stuff on your eyes.* But things had changed since then. The tension charging the atmosphere now seethed with the slow-burning intimacy rising from the ashes of their earlier discord.

Floundering, she said, "You're a good dancer, Liam."

It was a lie, a last-ditch effort to keep control of a situation already too far gone to be reclaimed, and she knew it. Except when they stumbled over each other's feet, the best they could accomplish was to sway on the spot to the music. But it didn't matter. It was enough to be in his arms, to feel his thighs nudging against hers. To drown in his gaze turned sultry blue with passion and to realize with delicious shock that he was aroused by her nearness and helpless to hide the fact.

Drawing her tighter into his embrace, he said unsteadily, "Maybe this wasn't such a bright idea, after all."

But the way he continued to hold her told another story, and when the music finally came to an end and he said, "Let's go," she handed him his cane and went with him in the full knowledge that the outcome of their leaving would be vastly different from what either of them had expected half an hour before.

The night was still, the water smooth as glass except where the boat's wake flowed in a graceful triangle from the stern. At first, as Liam navigated the narrows at the southern tip of the island, Jane sat well to the stern, content simply to admire his sleek powerful silhouette illuminated by the lights on the instrument panel.

She'd pinned many labels on him since they'd met, not the least and most unflattering being that he was stubborn, difficult, obnoxious, and proud to a fault. Now it was time to admit to another, more risky truth. He was also sexy, virile and unforgettably, unabashedly masculine.

For years, she had remained immune to desire, had been content to drift through life, instead of becoming caught up in the mainstream of emotion which truly defined it. Tonight, though, with little more than a touch and a telling glance, Liam had awoken her to a different reality.

She had, she knew, arrived at a fork in the river of her existence, and the choice about what happened next was hers alone to make. One way continued her along the quiet backwater which, until recently, she'd thought she wanted; to uncomplicated tranquility. The other led to turmoil. To passion and fire and uncertainty. To *living!*

A shift in the angle of moonlight on ocean alerted her to the knowledge that they'd passed through the narrows and reached the calmer water in the lee of the island's westward shore. Except for the low purr of the engine, night lay quiet all around them. Except for his figure, tall and silent at the wheel, there was no one else in the world who mattered, and she'd waited long enough to let him know it.

Going to him, she leaned into his spine, rested her head in the niche of his shoulder, and slid her arms around his waist. His midriff was hard as iron to her touch, his skin cool and smooth under the fabric of his shirt. Splaying her fingers, she explored the definition of rib and sinew which shaped his chest.

He said not a word, gave not a single outward indication that he was aware of her touching him. But his heart raced beneath her fingertips and when she dared to slip her hands lower, over his flanks to the narrow planes of his hips, she heard his sharply indrawn breath.

Still, he made no effort to respond to her overtures and, suddenly unsure of herself, she went to back away, afraid she'd misread the signs which had seemed to spell such a clear message mere seconds before.

Only then did he move, killing the engine so that the night closed around them like a thick, concealing blanket, and leaving the boat to drift idly on the ebbing tide. "Don't you dare back off," he said in a low, husky voice.

Less a command than a solicitation, it spurred her to rash confidence. Boldly, she let her hands roam the firm, flat contours of his belly, and then, with unthinkable daring, to where his flesh rose hard and hot against the confines of his trousers. At her touch, a shudder passed over him, powerful as a tiny earthquake.

Aghast at her own audacity, she made to retreat to safer territory but, covering her hand with his and pressing her more firmly against him, he said hoarsely, "You can't stop now, Janie."

"I don't want to," she admitted faintly, the blood surging through her veins like wildfire. "Oh, Liam, I don't ever want to stop."

He turned then and pulled her hard against him. Supporting himself against the instrument panel, he nested her between his thighs with such intimacy that she could feel the pulsing urgency of him through the layers of their clothing.

Her own pooling response was no less intense. She had never known such hunger, such aching need. Yearning toward him, she lifted her face to his. He towered over her, blotting out the moonlight, the stars—everything but the shimmering expectation of his kiss.

He paused a bare millimeter from her lips. "I hope you know what you're letting yourself in for, Janie."

"I do," she whispered, tilting her hips against his in

blatant proposition. "You don't have to worry, Liam. I'm a grown woman. I can look after myself."

Brave words, and ones she was prepared to live by, at the time.

CHAPTER SEVEN

HE RELENTED then, and slanted his mouth over hers in a kiss so shattering that her knees buckled. Clinging to him, she opened her lips to the subtle persuasion of his. His tongue flirted with hers, teased the tiny crease at the corner of her mouth, and wove wickedly past her teeth to engage in a rhythmic thrust and retreat that left her breathless.

Meanwhile, his hands...sweet heaven, his hands were instruments of exquisite torture, bent on discovering every tactile inch of her. The straps of her dress slid away. Above the soft thunder of her blood, she heard her zipper slide open, felt the cool night air on her exposed skin. Felt his touch, his fingers warm and slightly calloused, his palm firm and possessive.

At her soft moan of pleasure, he inched her dress and panties past her hips and sent them shimmying down around her ankles. Naked, and quivering with a mixture of hope and trepidation, she stood before him, more vulnerable than she'd ever been in her life before.

And then his mouth was at her breast, creating a turbulence which stripped away any pretensions to modesty she might once have entertained.

She arched her spine compliantly, the better to give him access when he ran his hand over her ribs to her stomach. Beyond a momentary shudder of delight, she allowed him to track the delta of her hips with his tongue.

When he strung kisses along the slope of her thigh

and her legs fell slackly apart, no more able to resist him than any other part of her, she acquiesced and allowed him to divine with expert finesse the sweet, hot moisture she was helpless to control, unmistakable proof of her surrender to his seduction.

Past caring that her too thin body was laid bare to his critical inspection, that she was indisputably, shamelessly ready for him, she rocked against him, almost sobbing at the escalating tension which threatened to rip her apart unless he stopped…!

Yet *if* he stopped, she would surely die!

Couldn't he feel her heart banging wildly behind her ribs? Couldn't he *hear* it disturbing the deep silence of the night? Didn't he know that she was awash with gnawing hunger, that a deep and primitive throbbing born in the very center of her being was spreading sweet tentacles of destruction to the very tips of her fingers and toes?

"Oh, Li…am…!" she sighed brokenly, her whole body undulating with need as he tormented the one spot most sensitized by his ministrations. "Please, come to me…!"

He lifted his head at that and stared deeply into her eyes, his own full of dark fire. Deliberately, he unsnapped his belt buckle. Tugged his shirt loose from his waist. Took her hand and guided it to the zipper of his fly.

Gaze still scorching over her, he said, "I'm not doing all the work, sweetheart."

His words fell rough as gravel in the night. His chest heaved. A film of sweat gleamed fitfully on his face. He was, she recognized dimly, in the throes of his own personal agony, one only she could assuage.

She touched him. Delicately; nervously. Uncertain

of her ability to return a fraction of the ecstasy he promised her, she hovered over and around the taut shaft of his flesh until, impatient with her efforts, he wrenched open his fly and closed her hand hard around him.

He was...he was overwhelming! Magnificent!

Wonderingly, she tested the silken weight of him, stroked the heated energy of him, her senses suddenly so fine-tuned to his needs that she knew instinctively how to please him.

He closed his eyes. Inhaled sharply. Let his head roll back against his shoulders. Brought his hands up to her head and swept away the silver comb holding her chignon in place so that he could clench his fists in her hair.

Curling her fingers possessively around him, she leaned forward and pressed her mouth against the pulse throbbing at the base of his darkly tanned throat. He tasted of summer and she knew she'd never again know the smell of the sea and sun-warmed sand, or the lush, fragrant shade of evergreens, without thinking of him.

He tasted of surging, masculine passion and she knew, too, that there'd never be another man like him, no matter how many others might come her way.

And in some tiny, unprotected corner of her mind, she knew that what was hers for the taking that night was not hers to keep forever. It made her mouth greedy and demanding, her hands clever and aggressive.

Stifling a groan, he held her away from him and traced his fingertip from her breasts to the shadowed cleft of her thighs, a light, electrifying flight of movement which left her suspended midway between heaven and hell. Then, snaking his arm around her, he pulled her down beside him on the runabout's broad cushioned starboard seat and, as smoothly as if she'd been tailored specifically to accommodate him, he laid claim to her.

A spasm seized her, a contraction of surprise and discomfort so brief it barely registered before she expanded to accept the rhythm of his lovemaking. Locking her to him, he drove into her, again and again. And each time, she rose to meet him, gasping at the sensual shock of him, so full and vigorous within her; riding the sweeping crest of each wave, and falling with it as it ebbed and flowed around her.

I love you, she wanted to tell him, passion saturating her every pore and diluting self-preservation to a faint, irrelevant memory.

But she did not. Instead, she lifted her face to his, her mouth blindly seeking. And finding....

Oh, how she'd missed being loved by a man! Her entire body contracting with need, she yearned toward him, open, soft, willing. How eager she was, how ravenous!

But he was equal to the task of satisfying her. Gripping her hips, he lifted her to meet him and gave until she was openly crying for relief.

When it came, it was...it was like nothing she'd ever known before. Matchless...sublime...!

In the hazy aftermath, with the boat rocking gently and his arm flung heavily over her, the urge came to her again, to say *I love you.* They were so exactly the right words for such a moment; the *only* words to convey the emotions he brought to life in her.

But another sound broke the silence first, a dull thud against the hull of the boat, followed by a second, harder jolt. Jerking himself to his feet, Liam peered into the darkness and let fly with a curse.

"What is it? Have we run aground?" Feeling horribly exposed without his arms around her, Jane ducked down in the corner of the seat.

"No," he said, firing up the engine and steering the boat carefully astern. "We got bumped by a log, that's all. But we've drifted badly. Better get your drawers on, Janie, and cover up, before someone decides to do the heroic thing and come to our rescue."

Mortified, she scrambled to find her clothes. How quickly the romantic mood had been shattered!

Much later, long after the boat was tied up at the home wharf and her house lay in darkness, Liam gave up on trying to sleep.

He'd made love to her, for crying out loud! The whole nine yards! Without a condom!

Hauling his sorry rear out to the porch, he eased himself into the hammock and in the cool, post-midnight hours, grappled with the enormity of his actions. That a guy of his experience should have made such a colossal blunder was inexcusable on any number of fronts.

He knew she'd been hurt by his silence, after the fact; and at the way he'd ended the evening, with a curt "Good night," and not so much as a hint of lingering affection. Even a fool of his magnitude could figure out the reason her mouth had trembled when she tried to smile, and recognize the sad droop to her shoulders when she turned and made her way home.

She'd probably berated herself for being easy, and cried herself to sleep because he hadn't said the things she needed to hear in order to make her feel better about herself.

That was the whole trouble with women, he thought,

shifting irritably to relieve his aching leg. They always had to analyze everything and find reasons to justify their actions, especially when it came to sex. It was never enough to accept that, sometimes, everything came together and it just...happened.

That's how it had been tonight. He hadn't planned to jump on her. Hadn't intended touching her, even. She wasn't his type—too needy, too serious, too morally upright.

So how come he'd suddenly wanted her so badly he'd damn near climaxed prematurely? And why now, when his animal appetites had been satisfied in spades, did the thought of her, all slim elegance washed with moonlight, get him into a lather all over again? Why couldn't he just chalk the whole evening up to a combination of circumstance and bad judgment on both their parts?

Moodily, he flexed his leg, and scowled. He knew why. She had a sweetness of shape, a generosity of temperament, that aroused his deepest suspicions.

She was the kind of woman who crept into a man's subconscious while he slept or thought of other things, and took up residence there so that he was never truly free of her again. He'd surmised as much for days and now he had the proof to back up his theory.

The realization gnawed at him as dawn crept up from the east and turned the sea to mottled pewter. When reason should have prevailed, he wanted her. Even when fatigue overcame him but the ache in his leg prevented him from sleeping and the stubbornness that was his nature wouldn't let him take a painkiller, he wanted her.

And he knew he couldn't have her. Not again, not

ever. Because he couldn't give her what she really wanted.

"Where do you see yourself, five years from now?" he'd asked her, just the day before, when she'd served him lunch.

She'd looked at her hands, soft, pretty hands, made to hold a baby—or drive a man mad with sweet caresses—then glanced off into the distance. "I'm thinking of taking the B.C. Securities course, and getting into the financial planning side of banking. It should be an exciting challenge."

Exciting? "You sound about as pumped up about that as I'd be if I was facing root canal treatment!" he scoffed.

"It's a realistic goal. The other things I once wanted...." She shrugged resignedly. "They weren't meant to be."

"You're talking about children?"

"Yes." Her big brown eyes grew wistful.

"Hell, Janie," he'd said, "just because you're a widow doesn't put you out of the baby game. If having a child is all that important, what's to stop you from going after your dream?"

"Apart from the fact that I'm already thirty-one, you mean?"

"That's no reason. These days, plenty of women wait until they're in their thirties before they think about having babies."

Face closed, she hugged her knees and stared out at the waning afternoon. "If getting pregnant were my only ambition, I suppose it would be an option. But a child deserves to have two parents. That's one thing you and I *do* agree on."

"So get married again."

"Just to have a baby? That's no reason. Marriage should be about two people needing each other because they're in love, not because they want children, and I don't know if I'll ever be ready for that kind of commitment again."

But she'd been lying—to him and more dangerously, to herself. If ever a woman was meant to be married, it was she. Whether or nor she was willing to admit it, she was like the boat last night: drifting aimlessly and getting knocked around by whatever happened to cross her path. She needed an anchor, someone stable and reliable. Someone like the man she'd lost.

Liam could no more fill that role than a snake could pass for an elephant. He'd known it yesterday, and nothing had changed since then. So what the devil had he been thinking of, making love with her tonight? Apart from misleading her, he'd risked doing the one thing he'd promised he'd never do: father an unwanted child.

Well, he was paying the price now. From the way his leg was throbbing, cavorting around on the dance floor, not to mention the acrobatics on the boat, had probably set his recovery back by at least a month. He felt lower than dirt. The forbidden fruit had tasted sweet enough that he wanted more, which meant he was in trouble up to his armpits. And since he didn't trust himself to stay away from temptation, he was going to have to make bloody good and sure that she chose to keep her distance from him.

He only hoped that was all the price he was going to be called on to pay.

Only a hopeless romantic would expect that he'd show up at her door the morning after, bouquet of wildflowers in hand and some indication that he'd found their lovemaking memorable. Before they'd even made it back to shore, it had been plain enough that he regretted the entire incident.

She wasn't exactly proud of it herself. The abandon with which she'd responded to him left her covered with blushes. But to pretend it had never happened, or worse, to try to avoid each other indefinitely, struck her as absurd. Sooner or later they were bound to come face-to-face again, and she'd just as soon get it over and done with. Beard the lion in his den, as it were. Surely that was the most sensible way to put the whole business into proper perspective?

"I made a couple of cakes this morning and thought you might like one," she'd say. "Oh, yes, and about last night—it meant nothing, Liam, we both know that, so let's just forget it. No reason to let it spoil our friendship…no, sorry, I can't stay for coffee. I want to take Bounder for a good long run before it gets too hot.…"

So she persuaded herself, rehearsing her little speech until she had it word perfect.

When she arrived at his place, a series of thumps and muffled curses led her to the porch on the far side of the house where she'd discovered him once before, testing the strength of his injured leg. He was there again, with his back to her, stripped to the waist and wearing only a pair of shorts for a change, instead of his usual blue jeans.

Using the railing as a support bar, he was exercising his bad leg, swinging it up and out in a sideways motion, with some sort of metal weight strapped to the

sole of his shoe—a grueling routine, if the sweat glis-
tening on his shoulders was any indication.

There was something so innately private about the
scene that she froze, her one thought being to steal
away and leave what she wanted to say for another
time. Had the boards under her feet not creaked when
she moved, she might have succeeded, he was so im-
mersed in what he was doing.

But at the sound, he looked over his shoulder and
saw her. In the split second before he moved, a string
of expressions chased across his face. Surprise, chagrin
and outrage followed one other in rapid succession,
clear warning that she was about as welcome as the
plague.

Sucking in a breath, Jane braced herself for the storm
about to break. He wasted no time in unleashing its
force. "Since when did I give you permission to drop
in uninvited? This isn't a peep show."

Prepared though she thought she was, the cold fury
in his voice still stunned her. How could he speak to
her so, as if she were the enemy? They'd shared the
ultimate intimacy only a few hours before. He'd kissed
her as if she were the only woman on earth. He'd made
love to her, moved her to tears, lain exhausted and
replete in her arms. What was so terrible about her
seeing him now? "I know that," she said. "I just came
by to…"

"Shut up!" he spat. "Just shut the hell up and get
out of here!"

When she continued to stand there, poised for flight
but too dismayed to effect it, he yanked on the T-shirt
he'd slung over the railing and made a clumsy grab for
his cane. "Fine!" he snapped. "If you won't go, I
will."

But in his haste to remove himself from the scene rather than tolerate her presence, he stumbled and went sprawling.

She saw then what he'd been trying so hard to hide. Faded to pink, the disfiguring scars criss-crossed the front of his leg like shiny railroad tracks, starting just above his ankle, snaking around his knee, and running haphazardly up his thigh.

"Oh...!" Unable to stifle her involuntary gasp of compassion and knowing how he would interpret it, she clapped her hands over her mouth. Then, as he continued to flail around, she went to try to lift him—a futile gesture, given that he outweighed her by at least seventy pounds.

"Beat it!" he raged, swatting at her ineffectually. "I don't need your help and I sure as hell don't need your pity!"

"It's not pity!" she cried. "Liam, please! You didn't push me away last night. We were close, we shared so much. Why won't you let me help you now?"

Driven by fury laced with a good dollop of his infernal pride, he finally got himself upright and lashed out at her with a fresh volley of insults. "How like a woman, to try cashing in on a man's one moment of weakness! Just because I did what you so clearly wanted me to do last night, don't presume that you can now waltz over here anytime you please and shove your way into my life."

"Did what I wanted you to do?" Stirred by such gross injustice to an anger which matched his, she glared at him. "Who do you think you're fooling? You can shake your fist and deny it all you like now, but the truth is, you wanted to make love as much as I did,

Liam McGuire, and the fact that you were able to perform so admirably is proof enough of that.''

He had the grace to look embarrassed. "Yeah, well, it's not a mistake I intend to repeat."

"That's the best piece of news I've heard all day!"

"Is that why you came over here to begin with? To trade insults?"

"No," she said. "I brought you some cake. I thought...I hoped it might—"

"Popular folklore notwithstanding, the way to this man's heart is not through his stomach, honey," he said disagreeably, "so if you think bribing me with a little home baking will win you extra Brownie points and get me back between the sheets, you're sadly mistaken."

"Don't think of it as a bribe," she choked out, the hurt she'd so far managed to sidestep finally catching up with her. "Consider it more a payment for services rendered. And enjoy it while it's still fresh, Liam, because it's the last thing you'll ever get from me. As for getting you in my bed, I'd rather keep company with a scorpion."

"Then we're finally in agreement about something."

Oh, he was horrible! Heartless. Inhuman. And she was beyond stupid to have thought for a minute that she could appeal to his better nature, because he didn't have one!

She went to turn away, before he caught the gleam of tears in her eyes, but he was more observant than she realized. A shadow of remorse crossed his face and he sort of reached out as if he might touch her. Then, at the last minute, he changed his mind and simply said, "Janie, wait just a minute."

"Yes?"

Something of the hope suddenly springing to life must have shown in the lilt of her voice because he immediately reared back and muttered, "Never mind. It was nothing important."

She should have left it at that. Instead, devil for punishment that she was, she said, "We might as well get everything out in the open, and be done with, Liam. You're angry, not just because I came over here today but because we made love last night, and pretending otherwise won't change the facts. I don't claim to speak for you but what we shared meant something— at least it did to me."

"Don't go there, Jane," he cut in grimly. "Last night was…a mistake. It wasn't planned, it should never have happened and it won't happen again. And it had nothing to do with love. So don't go calling it by names which don't apply, and don't go looking for reasons to justify it, because there aren't any that'll hold up under scrutiny."

She'd hated it when he first began calling her "Janie." But now, his reverting to plain old "Jane" struck an ominously somber note. "I more or less arrived at the same conclusion myself," she said. "The difference is that I wouldn't have spelled it out quite as callously, nor would I have used it as an excuse to end our friendship, which is exactly what you're doing. I never took you for a coward, Liam."

"Sometimes, a clean break is best. The sole reason I came here in the first place was to be alone. The same's true for you. We were each doing just fine, as long as we kept our distance. Our mistake lay in thinking we could have the best of both worlds—be neighbors and recluses both at the same time. But it's not too late to reverse the damage."

"Not for you, perhaps."

He grew very still at that, like a wild animal alerted to imminent threat. "What's that supposed to mean? Are you saying you might wind up…?"

"Pregnant?" Her attempted laugh struck a shrill, unpleasant note to the ear. "Isn't it a bit late for you to be asking me that?"

He lowered his eyes and made a big production of examining his feet. "Did you do anything to prevent the possibility?"

"No! Did you?"

"You know I didn't. But you could be on the pill, or something."

"I'm afraid not. Until you, I've never been with any other man except my husband." She swallowed, suddenly overcome with grief, less for Derek's untimely death than for its attendant losses. "It was different with him. He'd never have…there was never anything like this, the morning after. He loved me."

"Is that my cue to say the three big words? Is that what you're driving at?"

"No," she said sadly. "The only thing worse than sleeping with someone you don't love is lying about it and pretending feelings which aren't there."

"That's a relief! But it hardly answers my original question. *Could* you be pregnant?"

"I guess we'll just have to wait and see. If you happen to bump into me six months from now and I'm big as a house, you'll know—"

"Cripes, Jane!" he exploded. "This isn't something to be taken lightly. If you find—"

"Don't worry, Liam, I won't come running to you, not when you've made your feelings so plain."

"Your being pregnant would change a lot of things."

"But not the most important which is that, given a choice, you'd prefer to have nothing more to do with me."

"If there's the remotest possibility...if it's that time of the month when you're popping with fertility, I want to know. Now."

"What makes you think you're privy to information as personal as my body functions, when you feel perfectly justified in lambasting me for having accidentally seen the scars on your leg?" she exclaimed, a red tide of embarrassment sweeping up her neck and flooding her face with heat.

He pinned her in an unwavering stare. "Answer the question, Jane," he said implacably. "Is it a bad time of the month to be playing sexual Russian roulette?"

"No," she said, appalled at how easily the lie came to her. "If unprotected sex was in the cards, it couldn't have happened at a safer time for me."

"When will you know for sure?"

"Within a couple of days." More embarrassed by the minute and hurt beyond measure by his attitude, she passed a hand over her face, as if doing so would be enough to wipe away her distress. How hard he was; how unfeeling! "Really, Liam, I find this line of questioning most upsetting. Have you no sense of delicacy?"

"No," he said bluntly. "But I like to think I'm not completely without decency. If you don't get your period when you're supposed to, I want to know about it. Last night, we were going at it like a pair of demented polecats. I'm not proud of myself but I'm will-

ing to face the consequences, unwelcome though they
might be.''

Going at it like a pair of demented polecats?

She'd been so sure she could cope with seeing him
again, that they'd somehow find a way past last night's
indiscretion and manage to keep their friendship intact.
But his whole attitude, from the squared-off set of his
shoulders to the flat, disinterested expression in his
eyes, to his blistering disparagement of something
she'd found memorably beautiful, overwhelmed her
with such pain and regret that she burst into tears.
''You insensitive brute!'' she sobbed. ''No wonder
you're here by yourself. It's not from choice, at all.
You probably don't have a friend to your name!''

''Oh, cripes!'' he muttered, and raked a hand
through his hair. ''Janie, look, I don't want to hurt
you—''

''Too late,'' she wailed, swiping at the tears. ''You
already have. The damage is done.''

''But it's not irreversible.'' He caught her hands and
stilled their frantic scrubbing. ''Stop mutilating yourself like that and listen to me. You're right. I'm a louse,
a jerk—''

''You're a lot worse than that!''

''You think I don't already know it? I had no business making love to you last night. I don't have a single
excuse for letting things get so out of hand. But at least
I can make sure I don't repeat the mistake, and if that
means cutting you out of my life completely, that's
what I'll do. It's time I was moving on, anyway. The
rehab has gone faster than I expected and I'm ready
for a bit more comfort and freedom than this place has
to offer.''

He blew out a breath and patted her shoulder awkwardly. "As for you, you're ready for another relationship, for marriage, whether or not you're willing to come right out and say so. But I'm not the man for the job, Janie. I've got my own personal mountains to climb. I can't take on yours, as well."

"I'm not asking you to. I've never even hinted that I was looking for such a commitment."

But the sobs continued unabated because in a moment of blinding truth, she knew that the only person she was fooling was herself. Liam was right. At some point over the summer, she truly had emerged from that long tunnel of personal readjustment and was ready to love again.

"Not in so many words, perhaps," he said, "but that's okay. There's nothing wrong with going after your dreams. It's the healthy thing to do. And if I had a grain of sense, I'd cash in on the opportunity because you're a lovely woman, Janie."

He tucked a strand of hair behind her ear and cupped her cheek in his palm. "But I can't give you what you need to be happy. My priorities lie elsewhere. If my leg doesn't heal completely, I'll be crippled for the rest of my life. You've been down that kind of road once and I'd never ask you to travel it again."

"Not even if—?"

"Not even if," he said soberly. "You've seen the way I am. Most days, I'm not fit to live with. You've got to know I'd be even worse if I thought what I'm dealing with now is here for the long haul."

"It won't be," she said, covering his hand with hers. "You've already come so far. You're going to make it. I really believe you are."

"If you're right, and I hope like the devil that you are, then I'll be back on the job, leading the life I love—one you wouldn't find acceptable. You've already spelled out the kind of husband you want, sweetheart, and I just don't fit the mold.''

His beautiful aquamarine eyes stared into hers, and she felt something shift inside, a tiny splintering of shattered hope. She knew she'd never again look at the summer sea without her heart aching at the memory of him and that, no matter what the future held, there'd never be another man who'd move her to the heights of passion she'd known with him. But then, there'd likely never be another who'd hurt her in quite the same way, either. ''You don't believe in mincing words, do you?'' she said.

''No,'' he said again. ''One thing you can always count on with me, Janie, is plain speaking. I don't believe in sugar-coating the truth, so I think it's only fair to tell you, I'm cutting things short here and heading back to Vancouver as soon as I've got my stuff together and made adequate travel arrangements.''

CHAPTER EIGHT

SHE had to get away, far enough that she wouldn't see him limping out of her life. Far enough that she wouldn't give in to the urge to run after him with a mouthful of excuses which were nothing but a cover-up for the fact that she couldn't bear to let him go.

By early afternoon, she'd packed the supplies she'd need to see her through the next couple of days, and set off for Bell Mountain. Though steep and difficult at its higher elevations, the trail began in wide, easy sweeps at right angles to the fall line. She'd started out later than she'd have liked, but still she reached the cave well before sunset.

Her grandfather had first taken her there when she was about ten. "Found this place when I was a boy," he'd told her. "Made it my secret hide-out. Camped out here for nearly a week once, when I was ticked off with Steve for netting a bigger salmon than the one I'd caught."

"But what did you do up here? What did you eat?" she'd asked, fascinated by the idea but never dreaming that the day would come when she'd also seek refuge there.

"Brought books and stole some bread and cans of corned beef hash from my mother's pantry, and a pound of butter and a sack of potatoes. Even built a couple of shelves to keep my supplies—over there at the back, see?—and built a fire just outside the entrance to keep the bears away."

It had been years since she'd visited it, but nothing had changed. Ferns and salal still draped the entrance beyond which lay the circle of stones where fires, whose ashes had long since been washed away by winter rains, once had burned. Even the cedar shelves, silvery with age, remained intact. On one of them a collection of shells were lined up next to a candle stub and a faded old photograph of a rock star she'd idolized when she was a teenager.

Unexpectedly, the sight of them and the shining innocence they represented, brought the misery she'd sought to escape washing back with a vengeance. Bell Island had always been a haven, a place where killer whales sported off the western shore, and summer storms swept down with brief and violent passion.

Liam would be like them and leave the same empty desolation behind when he went away. She wished she'd never met him, never come to know his fierce and private pain, or his too brief laughter. She wished he'd never touched her, never kissed her.

She wished she didn't love him.

With a little cry, she dropped to her knees on the rough, sandy floor, and wept for the truth she could no longer deny. This was not how things were supposed to have turned out. She had returned to the island to restore herself, spiritually and physically, so that she could make a new start when she went back to the city. Instead, she was full of heartache, and all for a man who wouldn't care if she dropped off the edge of the earth.

A warm, wet tongue lapped anxiously at her face. "Oh, Bounder," she sobbed, wrapping her arms around his neck and burying her face in his fur, "how could I have let this happen?"

*   *   *

The trouble with living on the island was that a man lost track of time. It just sort of flowed by, making it too easy to put things off until tomorrow, or next week, or whenever the spirit moved him. So Liam's first reaction when the single-engine float plane came skimming down and landed with a hiss in the cove around four-thirty that afternoon, was an irate, "Hell and damnation!"

He'd forgotten about Brianna's proposed visit. Had barely given it a thought, in fact, since the day she'd left the message on his voice mail. But there was no avoiding it now. Disgruntled, he hobbled down the ramp to meet her. If she'd come a few days later, he could have hitched a ride with her and saved himself the hassle of chartering a commercial pilot to fly him home.

Taxiing the plane to the wharf with her usual flamboyant expertise, Brianna climbed out and stretched, a gesture geared solely toward reminding him of her considerable assets.

Then, shoving her sunglasses up into her hair, she cooed, "Precious!" and latched onto him like a starving leech.

Doing his best to hold her off without toppling them both in the salt chuck, he stretched his face into the nearest he could come to a smile—no easy feat, given his black mood ever since the screw-up with Jane. "Hey," he said.

"Let me feast my eyes!" she gushed, unfazed by his lukewarm reception. "Well, *darling*, you look good enough to eat, so tanned and healthy and fit and all! Country living must agree with you."

"It has its advantages."

"And its drawbacks, too. Did you have to seclude

yourself in quite such a remote spot? I had one devil of a time finding you.''

"That's one of its charms, Brianna. It's too inconvenient for people just to drop in for a visit whenever they feel like it. How long are you planning to stay?''

Her laugh rippled through the still afternoon. "I only just arrived, precious! At least let me get my land legs back before you try to get rid of me.''

"Just don't want you to feel obligated to stick around visiting the invalid,'' he said, "especially since I'll be back in town myself within the week.''

She slid her hands over her hips to the hem of her short skirt, a direct invitation for him to admire the expanse of smoothly tanned thigh. "Don't be silly, Liam,'' she burbled. "I'm here because I couldn't stay away. And anyway, it's an easy trip down the coast from here to the city. Shouldn't take me more than an hour or so, which leaves us plenty of time for a nice, long visit.'' She hooked her arm in his and began a determined stroll up the ramp. "Aren't you going to invite me up to your little cabin, darling? I'm itching to see it. And I'm perishing for something cold to drink.''

"All I've got is beer or well water.''

She made a face. "Good grief, you really *have* taken to rustic life with a vengeance, haven't you? Good thing I brought along a few essentials. Wait here, darling, and I'll get them.''

She flitted back to the seaplane, as out of place in the setting as a brilliantly colored tropical bird. Warily, he glanced over at Jane's place. No sign of *her,* thank God, though she could hardly miss noticing the seaplane if she happened to come out on her porch.

He hoped she didn't. She might not belong in the

bigger picture but his perceptions had altered since he'd first decided that having Brianna show up would effectively put an end to any ideas Jane might be hatching about him and her becoming an item. Loath though he was to admit it, he'd come to care enough not to want to hurt her, and in light of what had happened the night before, he knew she'd take it badly if she thought he'd been stringing her along to keep himself entertained until a better prospect showed up.

Not that Brianna fit such a description. He'd met her about a year ago through mutual friends who'd thought they'd make a fine match. Fat chance! She was too dramatic and a damn sight too persistent for his taste. Witness the fact that, of all the people he knew, only she had managed to find out where he'd chosen to hole up.

"Here we are, darling, just the thing to wile away the afternoon. Hope you've got a corkscrew in your little shack, because I forgot to bring one."

"Is that such a good idea?" he asked, indicating the two bottles of wine poking out of the picnic basket she'd produced. "If you're flying out again before sundown—"

"Trust me, Liam, darling, I value my life too highly to jeopardize it by piloting a plane when I'm under the influence! So stop glowering like that and show me your little house by the sea. I must say, if the outside is anything to go by, it's not up to your usual standard of living."

"It's dry, more than adequate for what I need, and far enough off the beaten track to ensure total privacy," he said, then added pointedly, "Most of the time, that is."

"Not so very private, surely? I see another shack a

bit further down the beach. Anyone interesting living there?''

"No," he said, ignoring the way his heart kind of jumped around a bit. Jeez, whatever had made him think bringing another woman into the mix was any sort of solution to the problem with Jane? "Just another summer resident who's also looking for peace and quiet, so it's worked out very well."

They'd reached his place by then. Tucking her hand in the crook of his elbow with unmistakable satisfaction, Brianna said, "That's good. I worked too hard worming your whereabouts out of Tom to want to share you with someone else. I plan to keep you all to myself."

Not if I have anything to say about it, he thought. *I intend to have you winging your way back to town within the hour.* "Well, here you are." He stood back to let her precede him into the house. "Not bad, is it?"

"How…quaint!" She paused on the threshold, transfixed with dismay.

"Of course, it's a bit of a mess right now because I'm in the middle of packing everything up. It's served its purpose though, but I can't say I'll be sorry to leave."

"Small wonder!" she exclaimed. "Dear heaven, Liam, it's positively primitive! I don't know how you've stood it this long. Crack open one of those bottles, for pity's sake. I need something to fortify me."

Half an hour of inane conversation, with "darlings" flying around like moths batting against a light, was as much as he could take. "Tell you what," he said, almost glassy-eyed with boredom, "I've got a couple of traps out in the bay. How'd you like to take fresh crab home for dinner?"

But while the bribe had seemed harmless enough at the time, leaving Brianna alone turned out to be one mother of a mistake.

He supposed he was partly to blame. He might have managed to head off trouble before it happened, if he hadn't taken the opportunity, when he brought the boat back, to tie up on Jane's side of the wharf, instead of at his usual mooring spot.

He told himself doing this was to make it easier for Brianna to navigate the seaplane to open water, but the truth was, he was trying to hide the fact that the aircraft was there at all.

Under the guise of tying up at the new berth, he cast a furtive glance toward Jane's place. Still no sign of her or Bounder. Either she was taking out her annoyance with him by baking up a storm, or she'd gone out—maybe arranged for the guy who brought her supplies to run her over to Clara's Cove for the afternoon, though he hadn't heard another boat powering up to the dock.

Climbing ashore, he swung his gaze to his place, hoping to find Brianna ready and waiting to take off. No such luck! Instead, she'd parked herself in the hammock on the porch, and even from this distance, she was easily recognizable as a woman. Sheesh! If Jane *had* gone over to the mainland and happened to come back any time soon...!

A glance at his watch showed it was nearly six. As a concerned and responsible host, he was well within his rights to urge his guest on her way. If she left now, she'd be back in Vancouver in time for a fashionably late dinner on the town, an option she'd hopefully seize with alacrity when she learned there was no crab to be had that day.

Cheered by the thought, he trudged back up the ramp. His optimism, though, was short-lived. As he rounded the corner of the porch, Brianna let out a braying laugh and literally fell on her face when she tried to get out of the hammock.

"I think I'm a tittle lipsy," she giggled. "I feel *so* relaxed, precious!"

"Don't be ridiculous," he said shortly. "We've had only a glass of wine each, and the bottle's still half full. You can't possibly be potted on the difference."

"I was thirsty and you were gone so long." She licked her lips and swallowed, then making a supreme effort to sit up, looked aggrievedly at the empty bottle half hidden under the hammock. "So I finished the first and opened the other."

He grimaced, unable to hide his disgust. He'd over-indulged in his time, but never to the point that he'd lost control. Had she any idea how unattractive she was, with her slurred speech and her features so slack that her face looked as if it was made out of melting wax?

"Tipsy, my ass!" he snapped. "You're three sheets to the wind, Brianna, and small wonder! How the devil do you expect to fly in your condition?"

"I don't believe I can," she hiccuped, trying to use his legs as a climbing post and slobbering all over his knees in the process. Giving up the struggle, she slithered back to the porch floor. "I think I'm just going to lie down here and take a li'l nap to clear my li'l old head."

"Don't you dare pass out on me!" he threatened, the possible repercussions of trying to explain her co-matose presence should Jane suddenly show up too horrible to contemplate.

Jane...everything came back to her, dammit!

For about the twentieth time in the last hour and a half, he looked over to her place. Still deserted, thank God! But how much longer could his luck hold?

"I'll make coffee," he said, sidestepping Brianna's attempts to use his feet as a pillow. "Brianna, for Pete's sake...!"

The effort of trying to focus on him left her slightly cross-eyed. "Don't be mad with me," she whimpered. "I love you."

Oh, cripes! Helplessly, he shoved his fingers through his hair and considered his options. To say they were limited was a gross exaggeration. He had only one choice.

Grabbing her under the arms, he dragged her into the house. By the time he'd dumped her on the sofa, she'd passed out completely. "First thing tomorrow, you're out of here," he informed her dourly. "And if you're still incapable of flying, you can bloody well swim!"

Overnight, a front moved in from the Pacific. Instead of the pale lemon light she expected, Jane awoke to a green semi-gloom and the sound of rain dripping on leaves. Pushing aside the ferns at the mouth of the cave, she looked out on a morning draped in mist.

So much for her plans to climb Bell Mountain! Much though she wanted to put distance between her and Liam McGuire, she wasn't prepared to risk her neck or Bounder's to do it. She had her compact stove and fuel, coffee and food, fresh spring water not fifty feet away, a book to pass the time, and a dry place to sleep. She'd simply wait out the weather.

But after two days with no sign of a break, and the

only other sound beside the constant patter of rain the mournful toll of the bell buoy from which the island derived its name, she'd had enough of her own company to last a lifetime. Too many thoughts of Liam filled her mind; too many regrets, and too many hopes which would never be fulfilled.

His face came between her and the pages of her book. His voice invaded her dreams. His remembered touch inflamed her body. Furious with herself for ever allowing things to come to such a pass, she recognized that her haven of retreat had become a prison. Furthermore, although it wasn't exactly cold, the damp lent the air a premature touch of autumn that had even Bounder curled up in a tight ball with his tail over his nose.

So, when, toward evening, the mist cleared enough for her to catch a glimpse of the flat, gray sea below, she rolled up her sleeping bag and headed back the way she'd come, arriving home just after dark, dispirited, tired and muddy.

She fed Bounder first then, while she waited for water to heat, she changed into a terry cloth robe, went out to where the old zinc-plated bath tub hung on a hook outside the back door and set it down on the porch. Normally, because she was by nature a private person who didn't go around flaunting herself even in the privacy of her own garden, she dragged the tub into the middle of the kitchen floor, pulled closed the curtains and bathed in there.

But it was dark, and it was raining again, hard enough that no one would be out in such inclement conditions. And who, after all, cared enough about her to drop by uninvited? Liam? Hardly! He'd made it plain he never wanted to see her again.

So, tired and out of sorts with life in general, she threw aside her usual caution and chose to bathe outside by the light of a hurricane lamp set on a kitchen chair under the shelter of the porch. Fortunately, the tub was small, more of an old-fashioned hip bath really, with a high curved back, which meant she had to sit with her knees drawn up almost to her waist, but the water, hot and scented with lavender bath salts, came almost to her shoulders and felt divine.

Leaning her head back, she closed her eyes and inhaled the fragrant steam. Oh, she was ready to return to civilization, for all kinds of reasons, not the least among them the comforts she'd so willingly forfeited when she'd decided to spend the summer at the cottage. Tomorrow, she'd start closing the place up for the winter and make arrangements to go home. Maybe then, when neither he nor the memory of him was a presence next door, she'd be able to put Liam McGuire out of her mind for good.

On the third night of their enforced confinement, Brianna came racing into the cottage from the porch screeching that she'd just seen a wolf coming up the path from the beach.

"There aren't any wolves on the island," Liam said wearily, by then so beside himself with worry about Jane's disappearance that he'd long since stopped caring what she might think if she discovered he'd had another woman staying with him since the fog closed in. "Either your imagination's running away with you or you've been at the booze again."

"I certainly have not been in the booze," she exclaimed indignantly. "And I'm not seeing things.

There's a black...*creature* out there and if you don't believe me, go look for yourself.''

Only then did it occur to Liam that what she'd seen was Bounder. Surging to his feet, he hobbled to the door and yanked it open. Outside, a heap of wet black fur appeared out of the dark and hurled itself through the air with maniacal enthusiasm.

"You great, stupid, smelly lump!" Liam yelled, clutching at the door frame and narrowly missed being flattened as Bounder skidded to a landing.

From the other end of the kitchen Brianna started squealing again and ran for the frying pan. "Put that down before you brain someone," Liam told her, fending off another enthusiastic greeting from the dog. "The mutt lives next door and he's harmless."

"He looks rabid to me," she shrieked.

If he were, I'd set him on you! Smothering the uncharitable thought before he found himself putting it into words, Liam managed to grab hold of the dog's collar and subdue him somewhat. "Relax," he said, his thoughts funneling into one overriding urge to see Jane. To make sure she was okay. To worry about someone else for a change, instead of focusing solely on himself and his own problems.

No, not just "someone else." *Her!*

"If it'll ease your fears any," he told Brianna, "I'll take him back where he belongs."

It was the perfect excuse to go over and make sure that Jane had also come home again. After all, just because Bounder had shown up didn't mean she'd done the same. For all he knew, she could be lying out in the rain with a broken leg or something and the mutt was trying to lead him to her.

Not until he'd rounded the corner of her house did

he see the glimmer of light on her back porch. And what it revealed rendered him motionless. Even his lungs seized up. About the only thing moving was his heart, and it was going a mile a minute.

Restraining the dog with a firm hand, he froze in the shadow of the leafy vine rimming her porch and stared at the sight before him. Skeins of steam rising from the bath tub coiled around her, teasing him with glimpses of skin, of delicate limbs and slender shoulders. She'd worked shampoo into her hair and piled it in a soapy lather on top of her head. It made her look like some piece of Grecian sculpture, graceful and almost ethereal.

As he stood there, dry-mouthed, with his lungs fairly bursting for lack of oxygen, she tipped her head back to expose her throat and let water from a sponge trickle like diamonds from her chin to the hint of cleavage showing just above the water level.

At that moment, he would have given ten years of his life to have caught those sparkling drops on his tongue.

He also knew he was flirting with disaster. Regardless of the wisdom of such a response, he was full and aching for her, stretched tight as a drum to the point of discomfort. Every instinct he possessed urged him to go to her, to take her in his arms. If there'd been room enough for two in the tub, he'd have shucked off his clothes and climbed in next to her.

He'd be better off backing away as silently as he'd arrived and taking a flying leap into the cool, rain-washed sea. Better yet, he never should have come over in the first place.

Get back where you came from! his conscience ordered. *Stay the hell out of her life!*

But his legs, so long useless, had different ideas and propelled him closer.

He must have made a sound, or perhaps she caught the hint of movement just beyond her line of vision. Her head snapped upright and she clutched the sponge to her breasts.

Even then, he might have escaped undetected had she not called out, "Bounder, is that you?"

Immediately, he released the dog and tried to shove it forward, but the stupid mutt refused to obey, instead choosing to circle him and give off little yips of delight which put paid to his remaining incognito.

Snatching at the towel she'd draped over the back of a chair, she leaped out of the tub and covered herself—or at least, as much of herself as possible, which was to say all her most interesting parts. "Who's there?" she called out in a high, terrified voice.

"Just me," he said because, although self-preservation dictated that if he had a grain of sense, he'd hobble for the hills, conscience wouldn't allow him to frighten her like that.

Her face was a pale mask of shock, her eyes great dark blots of alarm. Stricken, he stepped into the aura of light cast by the lamp. "I didn't mean to scare you, Janie," he said. "I just came over to—"

"You creep!" she whispered, hugging the towel more tightly around her and shaking with aftershocks of fright.

"Yeah," he said. "I know. But it's partly your fault I'm here."

"And just how do you figure that?"

"You disappeared without a word, three days ago. And the weather...." He shrugged. "Heck, what was I supposed to do?"

"Nothing!" she spat. "Just the way you expected *me* to do nothing when *you* decided to take off in the middle of a storm!"

"That was different. You're a woman and—"

"I'm surprised you noticed."

He bit his lips to stop himself from smiling. "If I ever had any doubts, Janie, you've more than dispelled them tonight."

But she was in no mood to be softened up with compliments, however backhanded. "You made me jump through hoops, trying to please you," she cried. "You used me as your whipping boy because you were in a wheelchair. Worst of all, you made me feel guilty and inadequate for daring to care about you. And yet you think all you have to do is turn on the charm when it suits you, and I'll forget how you've hurt me." She drew a shaking breath and big, fat tears trembled along her lashes. "Well, no more, Liam!"

Her words hit home. "Yes," he said. "I've done all those things and more. But that doesn't mean I wasn't worried when you disappeared without a word."

"Oh, please! You don't give a damn about me! You made that plain enough the last time we spoke. If you felt anything at all, it was probably relief that you were finally rid of me."

The tears, turned gold by the lamplight, spilled down her face. He didn't understand why they affected him so profoundly. Women's tears usually gave him the willies. But a great knot of feeling unlike anything he'd experienced before rose up inside him at the sight of hers. Not passion in the sense he usually knew it, it stirred him to a different kind of desire, one that had him pulling her against his chest despite her objections.

Touching her was a mistake—the most grievous of

a long string of mistakes where she was concerned, especially just then with her wearing nothing but a towel and a mountain of soapy lather on her hair. But did he let her go? Did he put a safe and respectable distance between them? No. He stroked his hand up and down her spine while he mumbled all kinds of nonsense until the quiet grief stopped shaking her and she sorted of melded to him, so warm and soft and womanly and begging to be loved. And he, God help him, found himself more than willing to oblige.

He had to do something to break the spell, something that would relieve the crackling tension without crushing her feelings yet again. Holding her slightly away, he ran the tip of his finger through the shampoo stuck to his chin, the way he might have scooped frosting from a cake, and licked it experimentally. "Hmm, this smells a lot better than it tastes!"

"You idiot!"

But it wasn't what she said that precipitated his next move, it was the way she said it, with a little smile that trembled over her mouth and reminded him how it felt to kiss her. Oh, brother, he was in trouble, and wading deeper with every second that passed!

Desperately, he put her away from him, took the empty pail beside the tub and filled it with water from the rain barrel at the end of the porch. "You'll catch your death of cold out here. Let's get the soap out of your hair so you can put some clothes on."

She bent her head obediently. Trying like the devil not to dwell on the graceful curve of her neck, he rinsed her hair until it squeaked in protest between his fingers.

"You got another towel?" he asked when he'd finished.

She tilted one shoulder in a provocative little shrug that sent a shower of drops glimmering over her skin, and said, "Just the one I'm wearing."

A wiser man would have ignored the implicit invitation in her reply, but he was long past the point of wisdom. Far from dissipating, the aching tenderness she aroused in him turned to raw, uncomplicated hunger and before her words had cooled on the air, his fingers were skimming over her, unwinding the towel from her body until she stood naked before him.

His voice sounding as if he'd dined on rusty nails, he croaked, "Then it'll have to do the job."

She stood submissively while he fashioned a lop-sided turban around her head, her eyes never leaving his face. "Were you really worried?" she asked.

"Enough that I haven't slept for two nights."

She reached up to touch his eyelids, then brought her fingers down to his mouth in a touch as soft as a butterfly's wings. "You must be tired."

"Sleep's not exactly uppermost in my mind, Janie, if that's what you're thinking."

"Nor mine," she murmured, tugging his shirt free from his jeans and placing cool hands against his burning skin. "That being the case, would you like to come inside for a nightcap?"

CHAPTER NINE

HYPNOTIZED by the sway of her hips and the knowing little smile playing over her features, he went with her. In his willingness to follow the siren she'd suddenly become, he left his cane on the porch, but he was too consumed with a more urgent throbbing to care about the torment to his leg as he climbed the spiral staircase to her bedroom.

Vaguely, he was aware of gable windows jutting out from each of the four walls, and a sloping ceiling rising to a central peak like a canopy. Of roses in a vase next to a lamp on a night table, and a long white nightdress trimmed with blue ribbons flung over a chair. But mostly, he saw the bed, its brass rails gleaming in the lamplight—and her sinking slowly to the mattress and holding out her arms to him.

She smelled like something imported from Paris— exotic, faintly spicy, deliciously feminine. Her skin had the luster of pearls, as if she polished it with moon dust. And even as part of his mind was telling him what he was contemplating was a bad idea, another part was reasoning that he was only a man, not a god. There was a limit to what he could resist. And if she was willing....

But conscience, refusing to go along with such specious argument, continued to nag. *She's acting out of character. Only a jerk would take advantage of her in such a situation. Haven't you done enough, without sinking to this level?*

As if she sensed his mounting reservations, she cupped her hands beneath her breasts and offered them to him. That, and the way she looked at him, her eyes huge and soft with trust, almost moved him to tears.

He was not used to such artless seduction; the women he'd known before her were wise with a wealth of experience beyond anything she could begin to realize. They knew how to protect themselves from hurt. They knew how take. But she...she was dangerously out of her depth and too focused on giving with no idea of what it might ultimately cost her.

Again, vanishing sanity had the last word. *Which is why you should back off. Now!*

"Maybe we ought to talk about this while we're both still capable of rational thought, Janie," he muttered, gripping her by the shoulders and trying like the devil to stand his ground—no easy feat given that she immediately initiated an even bolder move by tugging open his jeans and closing her hand over him.

"When did talking ever get me anywhere?" she purred, punctuating the question with a row of tiny kisses sewn from his chest to his navel. "You never listen to a word I say. All you ever do is argue with me."

"Ex...actly." Completely lacking in conviction, the word rolled out of his mouth on a strangled breath. But how the blazes could a man be expected to retain control, with her creating mayhem in his most susceptible areas?

Folding in the face of defeat, he stripped off his clothes and holding her just far enough away that he could see the sultry droop of her eyelids, he taught her the folly of testing him too far. Deliberately, and with a dedication that left not a millimeter of skin undiscovered, he shaped the delicate curve of her torso, from her shoulders to her thighs, marveling at her silken perfection, and exulting in her abbreviated cry of shock when he found her so sleek and ready for him that a touch was all it took to send her over the edge.

"Liam!" she cried out in a thin, lost voice, her whole body convulsing in a spasm of pleasure. "Oh, please…please…!"

"Not yet," he told her huskily, determined that their lovemaking wouldn't be a repeat of the last time—furtive and hasty, on a boat rocking so hard from their hurried coupling that they'd almost toppled to the deck floor.

This time he would prolong the pleasure for both of them, but especially for her so that if, tomorrow, she did question the impulses which had driven her, at least she'd be able to justify them with memories worth keeping.

He wanted her stretched out beside him, lying skin to skin with him; wanted the purely primitive satisfaction of feeling the soft curves of her body adapt to fit snugly against the angles of his. He wanted to savor the sweet cream taste of her and when the tension became more than he could handle, he wanted to bury himself inside her and feel her shudder beneath him, time and again.

What he didn't count on was how quickly his own hunger would run riot, or how helpless he'd be to contain it. The usual remedies—mentally tallying his assets, running a checklist of his stock portfolio, freezing his body and his mind in neutral—none of them worked. The fire continued to rage, roaring through his blood with explosive force. He was fighting a losing battle and he knew it.

Groaning, he fell backward and lifted her so that she was poised above him, mindless to everything but the anticipation of her moist, sleek flesh closing around him.

She weighed next to nothing, her bones so small, her frame so slight, that the miracle of her, of her body's ability to expand and accept a man, or give birth to a child....

Give birth to a child!

Reality, sharp as a stinging slap to the face, succeeded where more proven methods had failed. "What the hell am I *doing?*" he groaned, casting her away from him so violently that she literally bounced over the mattress.

The silence which followed rang with reproach. Chest heaving, furious with himself, with her, with life in general, he lay with his arm across his eyes and wished he were anywhere but with her.

Eventually, she whispered, "I thought we were making love."

He didn't answer. What was there to say? That love had nothing to do with it? That she'd led him on and he'd been too bent on his own gratification to put an end to her seduction before things got so out of hand? That he didn't trust himself when he was with her, that he found himself wanting to say things which weren't—which *couldn't*—be true, and make promises he knew he'd never keep?

"Liam?" He felt her touch on his arm, tentative, chastened. "Was I wrong?"

"We weren't making love, we were playing with fire," he said harshly. "Again. And I don't intend to risk getting burned a second time."

"Fire?"

The quiver in her voice stirred him to unreasonable anger. "Do I have to draw pictures for you, Jane? When a man and a woman have sex, they run the risk of making a baby unless they take specific steps to prevent it. The way I see it, it's bad enough that you might already be pregnant because I didn't use a condom the first time, without pushing our luck again."

"You're right, of course," she said, shrinking away from him as if she were somehow unclean. "I don't know how I could have forgotten—I wasn't thinking—"

Ashamed at taking out his frustration on her, he said, "Don't beat yourself up, Janie. It wasn't all your doing."

"Yes, it was," she said, and looking up, he saw her twisting her hands together in anguish. "I thought I could accept that things were over between us. I never thought I could be so…so forward, so aggressive. But when you came over here tonight, even though I wanted to be angry with you, I realized…well, the truth is, Liam, my feelings for you have…gone far beyond what I expected. It's the reason I ran away…and also the reason I came back again."

He flung up one hand, as if that would be enough to change the direction of her thoughts. "Oh, no! Stop right there, Jane! The decisions you make have nothing to do with me, any more than mine have to do with you. I thought we both understood that."

"Things change sometimes, whether or not we want them to."

"But not this." As if he'd suddenly found himself lying on a bed of nails, he leaped up and began flinging on his clothes. "Listen to me, Janie, we've had this conversation before. You're the kind of woman made to be with a man and you're ready to start over with someone new, but you'd never have given me a second look if it weren't that I'm the only specimen to be found in these parts. Once you're back in the city and can take your pick, you'll be glad you didn't settle for less than you deserve—which is what you'd be getting with a guy like me."

"Selling yourself short isn't going to change my mind," she said. "I saw the way you looked at me out there on the porch. I know how you kissed me. I know that you wanted me as badly as I wanted—as I *still* want you. And I know, too, that you're afraid to let anyone see that you're capable of tenderness. But I learned differently tonight, Liam. You can deny it all you like, but what's happening between us isn't just a one-sided affair nor is it just about sex, and nothing you say now will convince me otherwise. You care about me, whether or not you dare to admit it."

When a woman was able to read him this clearly, he was in worse trouble than he thought. "I care about your dog, too," he blustered. "But that doesn't mean I want to marry the mutt."

"Who mentioned marriage? I'm talking about feelings, about *love!*"

"Oh, jeez!" He could feel the sweat popping out on his forehead. He'd soon be drowning in the stuff if he didn't put an end to the conversation! How had he let things come to such a pass? He prided himself on being adept at spotting problems before they occurred and at heading them off, but if tonight was anything to go by, he needed a refresher course in the worst way.

"This isn't about love," he said, thumping his fist on the bed rail to emphasize each word, in case she didn't get the message he was determined to deliver, "so get the idea out of your mind once and for all. You're not in love with me, and I'm sure as hell not in love with you."

"Shouting at me isn't going to alter anything," she said mildly.

Stymied, he threw his hands up in the air. He'd have preferred not to be cruel, but she left him no other option. "Then maybe this will. Get dressed and come with me, Jane. There's someone I want you to meet."

It was the longest night of her life. The longest, and the most painful. Withered by humiliation, she huddled on the porch swing with her knees drawn up under her chin, and wished she could cry. But the misery lodged inside her went too deep for such easy relief. She wished that she could forget. But the memories were too recent, too raw.

Eyes burning, she stared out at the night-dark sea, but what she saw was a reenactment of the scene which took place in his cottage.

"This is Brianna," he'd said. "She's been staying with me for a couple of days."

Speechless with shock, she'd stared at the woman lolling on his sofa and wearing one of his T-shirts and precious little else. Brianna: a name as exotic as its owner. Superior, self-assured, polished. Tall and curvaceous, with rounded hips and generous, perfectly sculpted breasts which made Jane's look like plums by comparison. With hair the color of eighteen-carat gold, and long-lashed eyes which skimmed over Jane as if she amounted to nothing more than a fly on the wall.

"Jane?" she cooed. "How quaint! I always associate that name with the books children read in nursery school. You know the kind. See Jane. See Jane run!"

At that moment, run was what she'd most wanted to do, but she wouldn't give either of them the satisfaction of putting her to rout so easily. Pride in ruins but doing her best to hide it, she glanced past Brianna's cool amused gaze to Liam's unsmiling face, and said, "There is the other Jane, the one belonging to Tarzan. I tend to relate more to her except that I've found trying to tame an ape to be a complete waste of time."

He actually blushed. "Brianna's leaving in the morning," he said, at which she'd known a moment of absurd and short-lived hope which he immediately dashed by adding, "And I'll be going with her."

"Going with her?" The question was out before she could contain it, hanging pitifully in the air like a limb severed from its body.

"That's right." With a smile as brilliant as the sun at high noon and just about as painful to behold, Brianna unwound her legs from the sofa and strolled languidly to where Liam stood at the kitchen counter. "We're flying out in the morning," she said, coiling an arm around his neck and batting her silly eyelashes at him. "Weather permitting, of course."

"Flying out how?" Jane shuddered inwardly at the edge in her voice.

Liam had used her and abused her. All the time she'd been hiding herself away, confronting her true feelings—and, yes, she might as well face it: wondering if perhaps he *might* miss her, *might* realize his feelings for her ran deeper than he'd first thought—he'd been with this woman.

Dear heaven, was whining the best she could offer by way of retaliation?

"The same way I flew in, darling," Brianna gurgled. "By seaplane. I'd offer to give you a lift back to civilization as well, except it's a two-seater aircraft.'' She bent a smile on Liam that would have melted the fillings in his teeth if they weren't so perfect that he'd probably never known a cavity. "Just room for me and one passenger," she said smugly. "So sorry."

So she had a pilot's licence, as well as the kind of sophisticated beauty that left other women at the starting post! Recognizing defeat when it was staring her in the face, Jane managed a shrug and turned to leave. "Have a safe flight," she said.

She'd been halfway across the porch before he'd wrenched open the door and come after her. "Jane, wait a minute!"

"What for?" she burst out. "So that you can humiliate me a bit more? I'd have thought even you'd be satisfied with what you've already accomplished."

"It's not how it might seem with Brianna and me."

She laughed, a horrible hollow sound like something wrung out of a dying creature. "I think you've both made it perfectly clear how it is with Brianna and you. If you feel a burning need to offer explanations, I suggest you go to her and try to justify why you kept her waiting tonight while you almost made love with me."

"I have never made love to Brianna."

"Of course not. Forgive me! You *never* make love, do you? You have sex. Or, as you no doubt put it to your like-minded cronies, you like to screw women as long as they don't expect it to mean anything."

Under cover of darkness, she blushed and buried her face against her knees at the memory of her parting shot. She'd resorted to vulgarity and defiled one of the most beautiful experiences of her life, just for the satisfaction of leaving him speechless.

The tears did come then, bitter and scalding. Why

hadn't she listened, when he'd warned her he wasn't the man for her? He was a heathen, a savage. Cruel and unfeeling.

And irresistible. The curve of his mouth when he smiled, the storm in his eyes when he was angry, the rumble of reluctant laughter deep in his chest—what woman wouldn't be seduced by them?

"But he meant more than that to me," she sobbed to the uncaring stars. "He made me feel like a woman again."

Strong arms to hold her; virile, driving strength possessing her; hot, vital seed filling her with the belief that life could begin over again: these had been his gifts to her and for a little while she'd known the deep joy of owning them.

But then he'd taken them away and left her sliding down a slippery slope to despair. To gnawing loneliness, much worse than she'd known when Derek died, because then there'd been mutual pain, mutual regret. Now the loss was all hers. Liam was going on without her, by choice. What woman with any sense would love a man like that?

He came to her just as dawn lightened the sky to the color of ripe watermelon fading into lemonade, the kind made from scratch. Bittersweet and cool.

"Why are you out here?" he said, dropping down beside her on the swing. "I thought you'd still be in bed, sleeping."

"No," she said. "I wasn't tired."

"You've been crying."

What did he expect? That she'd spent the night drawing cartoons and laughing her fool head off? He'd destroyed her, for pity's sake! Ground her heart to dust under his heel and not turned a hair while he did it!

"Yes," she said. "Not for the reasons you might think but because I've made an undignified spectacle of myself."

"Don't blame yourself, Janie," he said. "We tried something that never stood a chance of working. We weren't meant to be, that's all."

She ventured a glance at him then, at the fluid, masculine grace of his spine curving forward, at his hands clasped loosely in his lap, at the clean, proud line of his profile limned in morning light, and thought she had never known such pain as that which knifed through her at that moment. "Then why are you here?"

He took a folded slip of paper from his pocket. "These are numbers where I can be reached. I want you to let me know if you should find out you're pregnant. Promise me you'll do that, Jane."

"Keep them," she said, turning her face away. "I won't be needing them. My period started late last night."

Still, he made no move to leave. Unable to bear being so close without touching him, she leaped from the swing and paced to the railing. "Didn't you hear what I said?" she cried venomously. "You're completely off the hook, Liam. You can fly away into the sunrise with your stuck-up, condescending *wench* of a girlfriend and never look back! Isn't that what you want?"

"I'm beginning to think I don't know what I want," he said in a low voice. "I guess the only thing I know for sure is what I can't have, and I can't have you, Jane. You deserve better."

"Oh, save it!" She hurled the words at him, not caring that he saw the tears coursing down her face, not caring that his last memory of her would be when she looked pitiful and ugly and a mess. "I'm sick to death of being handed the same old line all the time, especially when it's nothing but a fine excuse for not getting involved. You fancy yourself as such a big man, so *macho,* throwing away your crutches and bearing up under pain at any price! So why don't you have the guts to face the truth now? Your unwillingness to commit to me has nothing to do with your not being good enough and everything to do with your monumental selfishness. You don't believe the little homily you're spouting. You've got too much ego for such humility!"

"Ah, Janie," he said, coming toward her with his hands outstretched and his face a study in bogus regret. "If only it were that simple."

Last night, an hour ago even, she'd have given the world to fly into his arms. But suddenly, the thought of his touching her had her raising her own hands and warding him off with such strength that he only just managed to keep his footing.

"The only simple thing around here is you, if you think for one minute that you can butter me up with kindness this morning, after everything you pulled last night. I want you off my property and out of my life, Liam McGuire. Now that you know I'm not carrying your baby, I'm sure you'll be only too happy to oblige me on both counts."

She didn't wait to hear his reply. Didn't show her face to the outside world again until after she'd watched from behind the curtain in her living room and seen the float plane lift off into the bright morning.

Two days later, Don Eagle came to pick her up and take her to the mainland. She didn't look back as the boat headed south toward Lund. She never wanted to see Bell Island or the sheltered keyhole of the cove where Liam had found her the night she went swimming, or the runabout where they'd made love, ever again.

Indian Summer was long that year, stretching well into October with days of soft blue skies and nights sharp with the promised sting of a winter not yet ready to begin. But not everything hung in postponement. Just after Thanksgiving, when the lie she'd told Liam on that last morning still hadn't evolved into truth, Jane went to her doctor for confirmation of what she'd secretly known for well over a month.

"No doubt about it," he said, reappearing minutes after she'd provided the required specimen for the pregnancy test. "There's a baby on the way, due around the beginning of May, if you've got your dates straight, which puts you almost into your second trimester. What took you so long to come and see me, Jane?"

Sam Burgess knew her too well, had seen her through too many crises with Derek, to be taken in by pretense. "Denial," she said.

"You don't want this child?"

"I want...."

Liam.

Abruptly, she closed her eyes against the vicious ache of longing that never went away. It had been nearly three months, and still no lessening of the pain of missing him. As long as she lived, she would want Liam.

"An abortion?"

"No!" Her eyes flew open in shock and met Sam's concerned gaze. "That never crossed my mind."

"But there's no husband, is that it?"

"No," she said. "There's no husband, nor will there be. I'll be having this baby on my own."

"Hmm. Does the father know that you're pregnant?"

"No. And I don't intend for him ever to find out."

"You're facing a major undertaking, Jane. And after what you've gone through over the last several years, are you really up to the challenge of single parenthood?"

"Loving a child, caring for someone other than myself, gives me a purpose in life. I don't see this baby as a burden, Sam."

"Yet by your own admission, you've refused to face up to the fact that you're pregnant until today. Are you really so sure that you're ready for the kind of long-term investment you're facing? Because if you're at all uncertain, there are other options besides abortion. There's a very long waiting list of highly qualified couples eager to adopt a baby."

Give away Liam's child? "I could never do that," she said.

"Think it over before you dismiss the idea out of hand. It's not a decision you should rush into anyway, and I'm sure, whatever you decide, that you'll put the child's best interests ahead of anything else."

Although he didn't come right out and say so, Sam's implication was clear enough. If she really cared about her baby, she'd make sure it grew up with two parents and a stable home, not leave it at the mercy of a mother pining for a man she couldn't have.

The issue plagued her as she stepped out into the busy midtown street. It was shortly after noon, and the sidewalks were crowded with people taking advantage of the weather during their lunch-hour break. Small wonder, then, that she didn't see Liam and would have walked right past him if he hadn't blocked her passage.

"Hey," he said, looking almost as disconcerted as she felt. "Imagine running into you. I thought you worked in the suburbs."

"I do." Flustered, she scrambled to find something cool and impersonal to say; something which would erase his last unfortunate impressions of her and, above all, not betray the secret he could never learn. "I...I had an appointment which brought me downtown today, though."

You fool! What if he asks what kind of appointment?

He didn't. Instead, he studied her quizzically and remarked, "You've cut your hair."

"Yes."

"It's short."

"Yes." Aware that her replies were baldly lacking, she attempted a smile, a disastrous venture because her lips, instead of curving upward, quivered pitifully.

"I always think of you with long hair."

You think of me? How often?

"I was ready for a change."

"Yeah," he said. "Change can be a good thing. So...." He rocked on his heels and raised his handsome eyebrows. "How've you been?"

"Just fine," she said, clutching her handbag to her middle, even though the loose-fitting jacket of her suit camouflaged any hint of her pregnancy.

"And the mutt?"

"He's fine, too. And you?"

"Okay." His glance skimmed over her, touching fleetingly on her breasts, her waist, her legs. "You're looking well."

He was looking wonderful! Tanned and fit and delicious. "Thank you."

He smiled, and she thought her insides would fall out with longing. "You've put a bit of meat on your bones since I last saw you."

True enough. Despite the nausea which still attacked once in a while, pregnancy agreed with her. She had blossomed and he wasn't the first to have noticed. "Yes," she said, turning a half-lie into a half-truth. "I've been feeling much better lately."

"Uh-huh." He pulled back the sleeve of his lightweight bomber jacket and glanced at his watch. "You in a hurry to get somewhere?"

If she had a grain of sense, she'd plead another appointment and remove herself from his presence with all due speed, before she melted in a pool of yearning at his feet. But discretion had never been her strong point when it came to Liam. She was drawn to him as inevitably as the tide yielded to the pull of the moon and sun. "Not particularly."

"Well, I've got half an hour before I head out to the airport. Care to join me for a bite to eat?"

"You're leaving town?"

Why did it matter? He might as well be living in China for all the good it did her.

"Yeah." Another smile, even more disarming than the last. "I'm back on the job, and as good as new. No cane, see? I could manage a cha-cha if I had to, no problem."

That he could dredge up a reminder of that night they'd danced and made love—and speak of it so lightheartedly…! "You must be very happy."

"About some things," he said ambiguously, stepping back to allow a group of pedestrians to get past, then closing in on her again and taking her arm. "Look, this isn't the best place to hold a conversation. Let me buy you a hamburger or something while I still have time."

Decline! The longer you're in his company, the greater the chance that you'll say or do something to arouse his suspicions. What if you have to throw up? What if he notices your skirt is so tight around the waist that the zipper doesn't quite close anymore?

Seeing her hesitation, he made the decision for her and steered her toward the revolving door of a hotel next to the medical building. "Come on, Janie. Just because you've put on a few pounds doesn't mean you can afford to miss meals."

But instead of leaving her to make her own way inside the hotel, he crowded into the same pie-shaped section of the door, and for a few, too brief seconds, they were alone in their own tiny glass-enclosed world.

She could feel his body heat, detect a faint whiff of his aftershave, something he'd never used on the island. His breath ruffled the back of her hair, lifting the short tendrils at the nape of her neck. If only she could stop time; if only the door mechanism would break down and trap them together for hours; if only she could have him to herself for just one night and know again the fluttering ecstasy that was worth dying for, if that was the price God asked…!

Stop it! There are no "if only's" with him! He's part of the past.

But while her brain was once again fully operational, her body lagged far behind, inclining itself toward him like a flower desperate to feel the warmth of the sun. It was all she could do not to fling her arms around his knees and implore him not to leave her again. *You said, the night after we made love, that if I was pregnant, it would change everything. Well, I am, Liam. We're going to have a baby.*

Blackmail. Even the thought of it was dirty and disgusting.

"I'd take you upstairs to the restaurant," he said apologetically, "but I'm flying out at two so I'm afraid it'll have to be the coffee shop instead."

"That's fine. I'm really not hungry."

In fact, she'd be lucky if she could choke down a single crumb, her stomach was in such an uproar.

He found them a booth at the back of the room and waited until the clubhouse sandwiches they'd ordered had arrived before he said, "You mentioned you've been feeling better lately. Does that mean you've been ill?"

"No," she said, too quickly, too nervously.

He noticed. She could tell by the alert gaze he turned on her. "Is it...have you met someone?"

She looked down at her fingers, clenched in her lap, because to have continued meeting his candid gaze was more than she could endure. How could he ask such a question, when she'd poured out her heart to him, his last night on Bell Island? Did he think she was so flighty, so shallow, that she could simply switch off her feelings in the space of a few weeks? Or was he hoping to ease his own conscience for having thrown Brianna in her face the way he did?

"Jane?"

"Yes," she said, flinging him a defiant glance. "As a matter of fact, I have." And under cover of the table, she pressed a gentle hand to her womb.

"Is it serious?"

"Very."

He went to take another bite of his sandwich, then changed his mind. "This is missing something. Or else I'm not as hungry as I thought."

"Mine's delicious," she said. Another lie, but so minor compared to the whoppers she'd already told, and who was counting?

"This man you've met...." He paused, and fidgeted with his coffee cup. "You plan to marry him?"

"Let's just say that it's a permanent arrangement."

"Well!" He ran a finger inside his collar and cleared his throat. "In that case, congratulations. I'm glad things have worked out so well for you."

"And what about you, Liam?" she asked. "Is the lovely Brianna still a factor in your life?"

He looked a little taken aback by her acid tone. "Not significantly."

"She's one of many, you mean?"

"If you're talking about acquaintances, yes. If you're asking me if we're involved in a meaningful relationship, the answer's no. We never were, and we never will be. I don't have the time, for a start, and even if I did, she's not my type. But speaking of the time...." He checked his watch and signaled for the bill. "My flight's overbooked. I should run if I don't want to find they've given my seat to someone else."

He stood up and she'd have done the same if she'd had any faith in her legs's ability to support her. But the strain of keeping up appearances had taken its toll. She was trembling from head to foot and so close to losing her lunch that she wasn't sure she could make it to the ladies' room before she disgraced herself.

Through a haze of misery, she watched as he paid for their meal and exchanged pleasantries with their waitress. Then he turned to her again and for once seemed at a loss for words. Several times he started to say something, then changed his mind.

In the end, he settled for giving her a swift kiss on the cheek and said, "Goodbye, Jane. And good luck."

She hadn't watched him leave her the last time and she didn't watch him leave now. Even if she'd wanted to, she wouldn't have been able to see him. She was too blinded by tears.

CHAPTER TEN

IN THE old days, he'd have viewed three weeks off the Caribbean coast of Venezuela as a bonus, one he more than deserved for those times he'd found himself working at the bottom of a North Sea rig in the teeth of a winter gale. But this time, not even the foreign charm of Venezuela had been enough to fire him up with the old enthusiasm. Too often, his thoughts had turned to home, and that left him badly rattled. "Home" wasn't a word he'd ever invested with much meaning, until recently.

The South American job itself had been a piece of cake. No serious structural failure to worry about, no deep-sea diving, just straightforward inspection from a Remote Operating Vehicle and a mountain of written reports and drawings to present at meetings. From a professional standpoint, he'd scored big and put to rest any doubts anyone might have harbored about Liam McGuire being finished as a result of that accident in the Middle East.

For him, though, the old thrill was gone. For the first time ever, he'd boarded his flight back to Canada feeling oddly dissatisfied. Fifty years from now, when he was either pushing up daisies or getting ready to celebrate his ninetieth birthday, who'd give a damn that once he'd been on the cutting edge of sub-sea oil rig platform design? What kind of legacy was that for a man to hang his life on, if no one he'd ever cared about was left to take pride in his accomplishments?

Which brought him to the real heart of the problem: Jane. Too often when he should have been concentrating on other things, she'd come sneaking into his thoughts, and try as he might, he hadn't been able to shake her.

No use reminding himself she was doing exactly what he'd told her to do—namely, getting on with her life. No use, either, chalking up all the reasons she was better off without him. Whichever way he looked at it, he always came back to the same conclusion. He'd screwed up with her. Badly.

The question which hounded him all the time he was away was, had he left it too late to rectify matters?

By the time the edge of Stanley Park tilted into view as the jet banked prior to its final approach to Vancouver International, he knew he'd have no peace until he found out.

She wasn't listed in the phone book, but locating her was simple enough. He started phoning around as soon as the banks opened for business the day after he got home, hit pay dirt with the third call, and made an appointment through her assistant for four that afternoon.

"Smith," he said, when asked to give his name and the nature of his business. "John Smith. I want to discuss a short-term loan on a piece of property I'm thinking of buying."

He found the small branch headquarters easily enough, tucked between a florist and a deli, in a pleasant strip mall lined with flowering cherry trees laid bare by the late autumn winds. The entire wall of her office facing the main area of the bank was glass, so even though her door was closed, he spotted her at once.

Under cover of the newspaper he'd bought, he observed her. She sat behind her desk, talking on the phone. He wished there was another explanation for the relief which washed over him when he saw she wore no ring on her left hand, but the plain fact was, his biggest fear had been that he'd find her already engaged, or worse, married, to the faceless competition she'd mentioned at lunch that day, three weeks before.

If she were his, he'd put a ring on her finger! Hang a Sold sign around her neck, if that's what it took to keep other men away, because they were surely beating a path to her door. Unlike the person he'd met on Bell Island, content with simple pleasures, here on home ground she was cool, assured, professional; a well-dressed, beautiful woman very much in sync with the upscale community in which she worked.

It was too easy to picture her choosing wine at the specialty liquor store beside the jeweler's, or stopping in at the French butcher shop across the street to pick up some gourmet item to serve to her new man for dinner when he stopped by her house that night.

She'd have candles on the table and flowers she'd bought from the shop next door. There'd be a fire in the living room, with the mutt stretched out on the hearth rug, snoring like a locomotive.

She'd change out of the smart cranberry-colored suit she was presently wearing into something long and slinky. And he, Mr. Perfect-Whoever-He-Was, would raise his glass in a toast and, after they'd eaten, take her to the bedroom and—

Slapping the newspaper closed, Liam swung on his heel and approached the reception desk where a nameplate identified the spit-and-polished youngster barely old enough to shave as Creed Anderson. "I have a four o'clock appointment with Ms. Ogilvie."

Creed—what kind of name was *that* to lay on a kid?—consulted the day planner on his desk. "Mr. Smith? Please have a seat, and I'll let her know you're here."

A few minutes later, he came to where Liam had resumed hiding behind his newspaper. "Ms. Ogilvie will see you now, Mr. Smith."

Bracing himself and still not sure exactly why he'd come, Liam got to his feet and approached the door. She looked up, a pleasant, business-like smile curving her mouth. Was almost on her feet before it registered that the man confronting her was no more John Smith than she was Pocahontas.

Recognizing him, she turned so pale he thought she was going pass out, and fell back into her chair, the hand she'd extended to greet him clapped to her chest.

"John Smith?" she said dazedly. *"John Smith?"*

Liam shrugged and aimed what he hoped was a winning smile her way. "It was the best I could come up with on short notice."

"Why did you need to come up with anything? Why didn't you just give your real name?"

"I wasn't sure you'd see me, and from the way you're reacting, I think I was right."

In fact, she looked shattered, all the poise he'd been admiring but a moment before reduced to hollow-eyed shock. Still with her hand clutched to her heart, she said, "Why are you here?"

Uninvited, he sat in the chair across from her and planted both elbows on her desk. "Because I couldn't stay away."

"Why *not?*"

There was such an air of desperation in the question that if he hadn't known there was no earthly reason for it, he'd have thought she was afraid of him. "Because," he said carefully, "I've been thinking about you. A lot."

"Because you ran into me the other week, you mean?"

"Longer than that." He drummed his fingers on the table and faced up to something he'd been denying for the better part of three months. "You've never been anything but completely honest with me, Jane. It's one of the things I admire the most about you. I don't believe you could lie to me if your life depended on it, and I think it's about time I found the guts to deliver the truth to you. So no, not because I ran into you the other week. You've been on my mind since the day I left Bell Island."

"But that isn't necessary!" she protested weakly, looking positively devastated by remarks he'd intended as a compliment. "I'm fine, really. You have no reason to feel guilty."

"It isn't a question of necessity or guilt, Janie," he said. "It's a question of realizing I was a fool to walk out of your life the way I did, and of rectifying the situation." He took a deep breath and steepled his fingers. Concentrating on their mirror image in the polished surface of the desk, he plunged to the heart of the matter. "And of wondering how big a part this new man plays in your life."

"New man?"

"The one you mentioned, when we had lunch."

"Oh, *him...!*"

The slightly hysterical edge in her voice clued him in to the fact that something wasn't computing the way it should.

"Yeah, him," he said, eyeing her narrowly. "Surely

you haven't forgotten? You said he was here for the duration. 'Permanent' was the word I believe you used.''

"Well, he was—*is!*''

She was lying! If the two spots of color on her cheeks hadn't been a dead giveaway, the hunted look in her eyes was. And since it was so completely out of character for her, the big question begging to be answered was, why? "Where'd you meet him?" he said, affecting idle curiosity.

"Here," she said, the word spilling out of her mouth so quickly, it might have been laced with strychnine.

"At the bank?"

"Yes, that's right. At the bank."

"I'd like to meet him," he said. "Introduce us. After all, Janie, any friend of yours is a friend of mine."

If possible, her expression grew even more hunted. "He's not here today."

"Why not?"

Practically hyperventilating, she said, "He's on holiday this week."

"Gee, that's too bad." He subjected her to another close scrutiny. Nervously enough to pull it apart at the seams, she clutched her jacket across her breasts— fuller now than they'd been the night she'd offered them to him with such sweet innocence. "But at least it frees you to have dinner with me."

"Oh, I couldn't possibly!" she exclaimed.

"Why not? You had lunch with me the other week without coming to any great harm. Why not dinner now?"

"Bounder," she said. "I can't leave Bounder. He...barks when I'm not home, and disturbs the neighbors."

"So you never leave him alone at night?"

"Never."

"What about all day when you're at work?"

"It only happens at night."

He'd hadn't the first idea what was really going on, but one thing he knew for sure. His earlier suspicion was right on target. "You're stonewalling me, Janie," he said, leaning across the desk and pinning her in his gaze.

Her desperate bravado seeped away faster than air from a punctured balloon. "Yes," she whispered.

"Why, darlin'?"

Her eyes, always beautiful, always mirrors of her soul, were bright with unshed tears. "I can't tell you."

"After everything we've gone through together, you can tell me anything. Don't you know that?"

"Not this," she said. "Here isn't the time or the place."

Outside her office, a metal sliding door clanged into place as the bank closed up for the day. Creed snapped off his computer and shoved a bunch of papers into his desk drawer. The big overhead lights went out.

Swinging his attention back to her, Liam said, "Then let's go somewhere else. Let me drive you home."

"I have my own car out back," she said, shying away from him as if he'd suggested they commit gross indecencies on the brick-paved sidewalk outside and invite the whole community to watch. "And a few loose ends of business to tie up here."

More determined than ever to get to the bottom of whatever was causing her to act so strangely, he got to his feet. "Okay. If not today, then when?"

"...Soon...."

"I'll call you tomorrow. What's your phone number?"

"Never mind," she said. "Just leave a message here and I'll get back to you."

Like a swimmer diving into the open jaws of a great white shark she would! "Have it your way."

Backing out of her office, he hot-footed it past the security guard and out through the main doors to where he'd left his car. Nosing it out into the traffic, he found another spot across the street, under a cedar tree where the creeping shadows of dusk camouflaged his black Porsche at the same time that it offered him an unobstructed view of the small, well-lit area behind the shopping mall marked Authorized Employee Parking Only.

If she'd been telling the truth, there was no way he'd miss seeing her when she left.

And if she thought she'd shaken him off that easily, she was sadly mistaken!

Twenty minutes later, his patience was rewarded. He saw her clearly as she braked her late-model Taurus to a stop under the street lamp, then made a right turn toward the acre-lot view homes dotted along the waterfront.

Giving her a hundred yard head start, he pulled out after her.

She was still shaking when she got home. Shaking and almost sick to the stomach from being stuffed too tightly into the suit which had been a full size too large when she'd bought it a month ago. With a sigh of relief, she stepped out of the skirt and stroked the convex curve of her abdomen.

There was no getting away from the obvious: it was

maternity wear from here on. She had a couple of out-
fits already hanging in the closet and if she'd worn one
that day, she wouldn't be fretting now about how she
was going to break the news of her condition to Liam.
He'd already have figured it out for himself.

Liam...! The shock of seeing him washed over her
afresh. When he'd first walked into her office, her immediate thought had been that she was hallucinating,
the result of too many fruitless hours spent pining for
him. Or else, it was some other man bearing a faint
resemblance to him.

Heaven knew, she'd made the same mistake a hundred times or more since leaving Bell Island. The set
of a pair of wide shoulders ahead of her in a lineup,
the tilt of a dark head, even a stranger's slight limp had
been enough to quicken her pulse before she realized
her mistake.

But although any number of well-dressed business-
men might have found legitimate reason to request an
appointment with her, there was only one who could
lay claim to those candid, blue-green eyes and that sudden, devastating smile. Only one who could move her
so profoundly with words she'd never thought to hear
him speak.

*I couldn't stay away...I've been thinking about
you....*

Blinking away another rush of tears, she let Bounder
out to the back garden through the French doors in her
bedroom, then put on a velour robe and eased her feet
into plush slippers.

*You've never been anything but honest with me. I
don't believe you could lie to me if your life depended
on it....*

If he only knew! The appalling fact was, she'd done

nothing but lie to him, ever since the last day they'd been together on the island. Worse, she'd continued to perpetrate the greatest lie of all, even though he'd given her every opportunity to correct it.

Well, no more! She would have to come clean, not because he'd said he'd been thinking of her—that hardly amounted to a declaration of undying love, after all, particularly not from a man with Liam's aversion to commitment—but because she had no right to keep the truth from him. Why had she ever thought she had? The baby kicking inside her carried his genes, as well as hers.

But she could not have told him that afternoon, not with half the eyes in the bank tuned in to the handsome visitor leaning across her desk. Not unprepared, with the words coming out all wrong. A woman couldn't just spit out "I'm having your baby," to the man she loved, especially when he wasn't in love with her.

Outside, the dreary November night closed in, bringing with it the rain which had held off all day. On her way to let Bounder in through the laundry room, she stopped in the kitchen and tossed a frozen lasagna in the oven. She was eating for two now, and whether or not she had any appetite for food was immaterial. She had her baby's health to consider—which brought her to the problem she'd been avoiding since Liam had shown up in her office that afternoon.

Sooner rather than later, she was going to have to decide how to break to him the fact that she'd been anything but honest with him. But the day's tensions had taken their toll. Lured by the blazing fire in the hearth and the soft down-filled cushions on her living room couch, she set aside her problems in favor of following doctor's orders and putting her feet up for a while. She'd waited this long to admit the truth to Liam, after all. What difference was another hour going to make?

She must have been more exhausted than she'd realized because not until the persistent ringing of a bell penetrated her dreams did she realize she'd fallen asleep. Disoriented, she staggered to her feet. *The oven,* she thought fuzzily, and was halfway down the hall to the kitchen before she realized the sound was actually coming from the front door.

Although she wasn't expecting anyone, Bounder was thrashing his tail back and forth, a sure sign that whoever was out there was someone he knew. Probably her next door neighbor, Iva Chapman, another widow, well into her seventies, who'd taken Jane under her wing when Derek died. She was also the only person in whom Jane had confided the news of her pregnancy, and had taken to popping over every few days to check up on her.

But the figure on the doorstep bearing a bouquet of pink roses and a bottle of wine was too tall, too broad, too masculine, to pass for a harmless little old lady with nothing but neighborly concern on her mind. He was too unmistakably Liam McGuire, and clearly not about to leave until he'd received the answers he'd come looking for.

"I know you weren't expecting me, but this can't wait," he announced, shoving into the house past an ecstatic Bounder, and filling her little foyer with his overwhelming presence.

Floored by his sudden appearance for the second time in as many hours, she gasped, "How did you find out where I live?"

"I followed you home. You're an easy mark, Janie.

You didn't once check in your rearview mirror, or you'd have seen me tailing you.''

"But why? We decided you'd call me at work and—"

"*You* decided, sweetheart, not I." Thrusting the flowers at her, he held Bounder off with one hand and hefted the bottle out of danger with his other. "At least I don't come empty-handed. Stick those in some water while I open the excellent wine I came across at that little mall where you work, then we'll talk."

"Talk?" she echoed, backing down the hall to the kitchen.

"That's right." He followed, tossing his suit jacket over a chair as he passed by the living room, and loosening the knot in his tie. And if that wasn't hint enough that he wasn't about to tolerate any more delaying tactics, his next words were. "It's show time, Janie. At first, I was prepared to humor you and put things off until tomorrow, but I've never been long on patience, a fact you're only too well acquainted with, and I'm afraid this can't wait."

"What can't wait?" Flustered, she busied herself finding a vase and trimming the ends of the rose stems before plunging them into water. Had he guessed she was pregnant, was that it? Was he going to blast her to kingdom come for deceiving him and depriving him of his right to the truth?

"Us," he said. "You and me."

"You and me?"

"Quit repeating everything I say, Janie," he said roughly, "and show me where you keep your corkscrew. Suddenly, I need a drink."

"In the drawer on top of the wine cabinet. Thank you for the flowers, by the way. They're lovely." And at any other time, she'd have been over the moon to accept them. But these definitely came with a price, though not the one she was expecting to pay.

"It might have taken me a while to figure out what I want," Liam said, uncorking the wine and taking down two stemmed glasses from the rack above the cabinet, "but now that I have, give it to me straight. What's it going to take to get rid of the competition?"

"Competition?"

"This other man. And don't bother telling me you're in love with him because you as good as said the same thing to me not three months ago, and you're not the type to change your mind that quickly."

Mutely, she stared at the rose in her hand. Had she heard him correctly? Was he saying that he...that he *cared* about her? The way she cared about him?

"Don't leave me hanging, Janie. Am I going to have to challenge him to a duel at dawn, or what?"

Slowly, she turned to meet his forthright gaze. "There isn't any other man, Liam," she said. "There never was. There was only ever you."

His jaw dropped. He set down the wine so abruptly that some splashed out and ran down the neck of the bottle. "I've never pretended to understand the working of the female mind," he said slowly, "but this beats everything! You've always been so straight with me, Janie. Why now...?"

"When I ran into you in town that day, you were so...on top of everything." She drew an unsteady breath. "You could hardly wait to get on that plane, back to the life and the work you love so much, while I...I was barely making it through each day, I missed you so badly. But when you asked if I'd met someone new, rather than admit my life had never been so empty, I lied. And I continued the lie when you showed up at the bank today."

"Why, for crying out loud?"

"Because I didn't want you feeling sorry for me."

"Sorry for you?" In three strides, he'd crossed the room and taken her in his arms. "Cripes, Janie, I'm trying to tell you I'm in love with you!" he said, almost smothering her in kisses. "How many ways do I have to spell it before you understand? I want you in my life."

"You want adventure and excitement, Liam. You've told me so a dozen times. And I'm the least adventurous or exciting woman you know."

"And it's taken me this long to realize I had it all wrong. It took you to make me realize I was hanging everything on a job that could—that almost did—end in the blink of an eye. And why? For the pleasure of coming back to an empty apartment and friends who suddenly didn't want to know me when it seemed I might wind up with only one leg."

He smiled down at her and tipped up her chin so that she had no choice but to meet his candid gaze. "Then I met you, darlin', and although I fought you every step of the way, you taught me to face the truth and not be afraid."

"Don't make me out to be some sort of saint," she cried, slipping out of his hold and spinning away from him. "I'm not perfect. I've made mistakes, too."

"Because you fibbed about having met someone else?" Sliding his arms around her from behind, he pulled her back to lean against him and splayed his fingers possessively over her ribs. "Oh, Janie, you're the only woman I know who'd see that as some great, unforgivable sin!"

Oh, God! she thought in terror. *Any second now and he'll feel the baby! I can't let him find out that way!*

Desperation gave her strength. Wrestling free of his hold again, she stumbled around the work island in the middle of the kitchen, safely beyond his reach. "Listen to me!" she wept, the tears she'd tried to stem scalding her face. "I've told you terrible lies."

"What are you talking about, Janie?" The teasing laughter died in his voice and left it somber with sudden doubt. "What have you done that's so dreadful?"

"I've kept the truth from you. A very important truth."

"Which is?"

"I'm…pregnant."

If she'd picked up a knife and stabbed him, he couldn't have looked more shocked. Eventually, he said, "Are you saying there *is* another man, after all? Good God, Jane, what kind of game are you playing here?"

"It's no game," she said in a low, ashamed voice, "and there's no other man. I'm carrying your baby, Liam."

"Like hell you are! I asked you, that last day on the island and you told me flat out that—"

"I lied."

"Again?" His laugh was vitriolic. "And what flimsy reason prompted that particular deception?"

"I didn't want you to feel trapped. I didn't want you staying with me out of obligation."

"Don't you think that should have been my decision to make?"

"Yes," she said, unable to look him in the eye. "But at the time, I didn't know anything for sure. I was hoping I'd find I'd told you the truth."

"And when you realized you hadn't?" The edge in his words was sharp as steel and just as cold.

"You'd made no attempt to get in touch with me. I never expected to hear from you or see you again. So I decided I'd have the baby on my own."

"When you knew how I felt about a child being abandoned by a parent? When I'd told you I was willing to take responsibility, if there was a baby on the way? Why, you...you devious little witch!" He thumped his fist on the wine cabinet and sent the stemware rattling like wind chimes.

"I'd have told you eventually. I know that now."

"Oh? When? Not this afternoon, when I gave you every opportunity. Not the day I bought you lunch, when you also had opportunity. And not tomorrow when you promised we'd get together and talk, because I'm willing to bet that was just another attempt to put me off, wasn't it? So when, honey? When the kid needed money to go to college? When he wound up in juvenile detention because he'd never had a father figure to lead him in the right direction and his mother never told him anything but lies? Or were you simply planning on dumping him on my doorstep with a note, when he became too much of a problem for you to handle alone?"

She lifted haunted eyes to his. "You know better than to ask me that, Liam."

"I don't know you at all," he said coldly. "I only know what you choose to show me and that, I'm beginning to see, is only the tip of the iceberg. Jeez!" Furious, he swung away and slammed his fist on the counter this time, hard enough to send Bounder slinking off to his bed in the laundry room. "To think you just stood there and let me spill my guts like a damned fool! I should have followed my first instinct and given you a wide berth. I knew you were nothing but trouble, the day I met you.''

''If it means anything at all,'' she whispered, her heart contracting painfully at the scornful disgust lacing his words, ''I was telling you the absolute truth when I said my feelings for you had changed. I love you, Liam. I've loved you for a very long time.''

He remained with his back to her, silent except for the breath hissing sharply in his lungs. And because she had nothing to lose, she did the only thing which might possibly have persuaded him to forgive her. She went to stand beside him and took his hand and placed it on the swell of her abdomen, so well concealed beneath the full velour robe.

''This is your child,'' she said. ''Feel him kicking? He's a living human being whom we created together. Can't we try to mend what's broken between us, for his sake?''

For the longest time, he didn't reply. But nor did he immediately remove his hand, and that gave her a little hope. A sigh shuddered over him and he seemed to be waging a silent war within himself.

At last, he pulled away and said grimly, ''I can't give you an answer to that, Jane, because right now my mind's spinning. I have to get out of here, be by myself, and sort a few things out. I need time to re-group, and I can't do it here, with you dogging my every step and hanging on my every word. I'm too afraid I might say something I'll regret in the morning.''

''I understand,'' she said, clinging to her control by a very fine thread. ''Probably neither of us should be making any decisions tonight.''

At the front door, he paused and looked at her. For a second, the thought crossed her mind that if she were to kiss him, he might relent and if he truly was in love with her, the hard edges of his anger would melt away. But the chasm of resentment and mistrust between them was wider than the ocean and too deep for her to dare try to cross.

Mutely, she held open the door and watched him walk away from her. Again.

CHAPTER ELEVEN

SHE walked the floor all that night, waiting; praying that he'd come back. When morning blew in, gloomy with rain, and still no word from him, Jane begged off work, so weary from lack of sleep and so heartsick at the mess she'd made of things that she couldn't face her colleagues at the bank.

Shortly before ten, the doorbell rang. Heart pounding with revived hope, she rushed to the bathroom to brush her hair before she answered. It was Iva Chapman, her next door neighbor. "I saw your car was still here, dear," she said, "and I know you're usually gone by nine on workdays, so I thought I'd better stop by, to make sure you're not ill."

"I'm fine, Mrs. Chapman," she said, knowing her red, puffy eyes belied her words. "Just taking a day off to catch up on some badly needed sleep."

Iva regarded her knowingly. "I''ll bring you some soup for lunch," she declared. "There's nothing like my home-made chicken noodle to make a body feel better and it's important for the baby that you keep your spirits up. Try classical music, dear. I've heard that helps, too."

Just after eleven, the bell rang again and once again her pulse quickened. "Registered envelope," the mail man said, holding out a clipboard with a form attached. "Sign here, please."

But he wasn't delivering a love letter from Liam,

only her new gold credit card. She'd barely closed the door before she succumbed to another bout of weeping.

At noon, Iva reappeared. "I won't stay," she said, bustling into the bedroom with a covered tray. "Eat the soup while it's hot, dear, and don't worry about returning the dishes. I'll collect them later."

The afternoon wore on, with rain spitting against the windows and the wind howling down the chimney. "He's never coming back," Jane sniffled to a sympathetic Bounder, who took immediate advantage of her sorry state to jump into bed with her and make himself comfortable.

When the bell rang again, just after four, she didn't even bother to check her appearance. Who cared if her hair was standing on end, the end of her nose was red enough to stop traffic, and she looked like the wrath of God?

"Hey," Liam said, when she cracked open the door. "You weren't at the office today. How come?"

She could have done what any sane woman would have done in the same situation, which was tell him to come back in an hour when she'd made herself presentable. She could have told him that, in light of his unforgiving attitude the day before, it was none of his business why she'd taken the day off. She could have informed him that she'd changed her mind and didn't want anything to do with a man who'd put her through more misery in one summer than she'd known in ten with her late husband.

Instead, she hung on to the door frame as if it were a lifeline and burst into tears.

"Oh, jeez!" he said, trying to inch the door open without squashing her bare toes. "I was afraid of this!"

"What?" she snuffled, the word emerging as little more than a watery snort.

"Something's gone wrong with the pregnancy and it's all my fault. I knew it the minute they told me at the bank that you hadn't shown up for work today. Sweetheart, someone should take me out and shoot me, but—!"

"The baby's fine," she wailed.

"It is?" His relief was almost palpable. "You're sure? I mean, this isn't another attempt to hoodwink me, is it? You wouldn't lie about something this important?"

"Of course I wouldn't!"

She tried to sound incensed, but when the best she could manage was a waterlogged hiccup, he continued to regard her suspiciously. "Then why are you crying?"

"You have to ask?" This time, her indignation carried a more authentic ring.

"Because of me? Because I'm a thickheaded clod with about as much sensitivity as a brick?"

"All that and more," she informed him soggily, catching sight of herself in the wall mirror. "It's all your fault I look such a mess."

"Sure it is," he said, scooping her up in his arms and planting a kiss on her mouth that would have melted the polar ice cap. "I'm a first-class jackass and I don't know why you give me the time of day."

"I don't know, either," she said, but she wound her arms tightly around his neck to make sure he didn't take umbrage and disappear again.

He carried her to the couch in the living room, cradled her in his lap and tilted her face so that he could look deep into her eyes. "Because it's a rotten job but someone's got to do it?"

How easily he brought out the sun in her life. A touch, a glance, his droll sense of humor—they were as much a part of the fabric of her love for him as the passion he aroused in her. "Maybe," she said, the ghost of a smile emerging through the tears.

He dropped his forehead against hers and she felt a shuddering sigh sweep through him. "Sweetheart," he said soberly, "I'm sorry I made you cry. I swore I'd never do that again. But the plain truth is, my feelings for you scare me to death and that's the only excuse I can offer for running out on you last night. I drove for hours trying to escape my demons, but no matter how far or fast I went, I couldn't outrun the one thing I know to be true. My life is nothing without you in it."

"But I don't fit the kind of life you lead. You told me that often enough last summer. You like challenge and adventure."

"And I get both in spades with you. Daring to admit that I love you is the biggest risk I've ever taken, and I can't face it alone."

"But you said you didn't want children. You said—"

"I said a lot of things except the one thing that matters the most. I love you, Jane. I'm through with chasing danger all over the globe. There are plenty of other ways of earning a living and I'm not exactly short of cash. I can afford to keep you in style. It's the things money can't buy that I'm looking for now. I want to live to a ripe old age with you. I want what any man of good sense wants: a woman like you to come home to. Don't ask me when I realized it because I'm damned if I can put a date on it. And don't ask me why I fought it, because I don't know that, either. Just try to forgive me and help me become a better man for you and our child.''

"It hasn't been all your fault," she said, almost drowning with love for him. "If I'd told you about the baby—"

"You would have, if I'd faced up to my feelings sooner, instead of denying them, and you.''

He put her from him then, setting her as carefully on the cushions as if she were made of the most fragile china, and snapped open a small green velvet box he withdrew from his pocket. "I want to do this right," he said, squaring his shoulders and tugging his tie into place. "You once told me that if ever I needed anything from you, all I had to do was ask. Well, I'm asking you now. Will you marry me, Janie?''

She could have done what any sane woman would have done in the same situation, which was ask him to save his proposal until she'd washed her face, sprayed on a little perfume, and slipped into something suitably romantic. She could have made him suffer at least a little bit, and said she needed time to think before taking such a momentous step.

But the irrefutable truth was, she loved him in all his cantankerous, proud, impossible glory. So she did what she seemed to do best these days. She burst into tears.

"Should I take that to mean 'Yes'?''

"Yes.''

"Then why are you crying again?'' he asked, clearly mystified.

"Because I'm pregnant. It's hormones.''

"Oh, jeez!'' He rolled his eyes in mock despair. "What will it take to cheer you up?''

"They do say actions speak louder than words," she howled, soaking the front of his shirt with happy tears and winding herself around him the best way she knew how, given the fact that their baby insisted on coming between them.

"I never was very good with words, anyway," he said, taking her left hand and sliding a ring blazing with diamonds onto her finger. "There, now it's official. Is there anything else I can do?"

"You could kiss me," she said. "I believe that's usually how a couple seals their engagement."

"Hell, I can do better than that, Janie," he said, sweeping her up into his arms again. "Direct me to the bedroom and I'll prove it."

He's a man of cool sophistication.
He's got pride, power and wealth.
He's a ruthless businessman, an expert lover—
and he's one hundred percent committed
to staying single.

Until now. Because suddenly he's responsible
for a BABY!

HIS BABY

An exciting miniseries from Harlequin Presents®
He's sexy, he's successful...
and now he's facing up to fatherhood!

On sale February 2001:
RAFAEL'S LOVE-CHILD
by Kate Walker, Harlequin Presents® #2160

On sale May 2001:
MORGAN'S SECRET SON
by Sara Wood, Harlequin Presents® #2180

And look out for more later in the year!

Available wherever Harlequin books are sold.

HARLEQUIN®
Makes any time special ™

Visit us at www.eHarlequin.com   HPBABY

If you enjoyed what you just read,
then we've got an offer you can't resist!

Take 2 bestselling love stories FREE!

Plus get a FREE surprise gift!

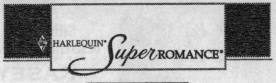